LOVE UNDER FIRE

JENNIFER YOUNGBLOOD
SANDRA POOLE

ARBOR
HOUSE

YOUR FREE BOOK AWAITS

Get Beastly Charm: A Contemporary retelling of beauty & the beast as a welcome gift when you sign up for my newsletter. You'll get information on my new releases, book recommendations, discounts, and other freebies.

Get the book at:

http://bit.ly/freebookjenniferyoungblood

PROLOGUE

*P*eyton couldn't help but feel like Cinderella as her gaze took in the opulent surroundings of the courtyard at the Webster Mansion. Twinkling white lights and thin strips of gauzy fabric adorned the gazebo and trellis, adding a dreamlike quality to the warm evening. A live orchestra played soft music in the background, and the tender scent of fresh flowers filled the night air. Stars shimmered brilliantly above, applauding the happy occasion of her upcoming wedding.

Peyton looked down at her exquisite mango-colored dress and couldn't resist swishing discreetly from side to side, loving how the wind whooshed underneath the silk fabric. She felt as buoyant as a balloon, soaring high and free, where nothing bad could touch her. It was still hard to believe she was marrying Carter tomorrow.

His mother, Kathryn, had been vehemently opposed to the union, but was starting to come around. This party at Kathryn's sprawling mansion was her gift to Carter and Peyton. It meant the world to Peyton that Kathryn was finally accepting her.

Peyton straightened her shoulders as she nodded and smiled at the mayor and his high-society wife. She straightened her back. A part of her wondered if she'd ever feel completely at home in Carter's glitzy

1

world of mansions, expensive cars, and spontaneous trips to Europe. It boggled Peyton's mind that Carter could just up and go anywhere he wanted when it had taken six months of planning, scrimping, and saving for her family to drive nine hours to Disneyland.

Peyton was sure there would be battles to fight when it came to the differences in their upbringing, but she was confident her and Carter's love was strong enough to see them through the rough spots. They'd weathered their fair share of storms already. She scanned the sea of faces, relieved when her eyes found a familiar face, Mr. Labrum. Her high school English teacher smiled and waved as he walked over and gave her a one-armed hug.

"Good evening," he said stiffly. "You look lovely as always." He pushed his inch-thick glasses back up on his nose and cleared his throat like he was about to deliver an important speech.

"BEAUTY, sweet Love, is like the morning dew,

WHOSE SHORT REFRESH upon the tender green

CHEERS FOR A TIME, but till the sun doth show,

AND STRAIGHT 'TIS gone as it had never been."

PEYTON LAUGHED. "THANKS ... I THINK."

"A sonnet by Samuel Daniel, born in 1562."

"Oh, I haven't heard that one," said Payton. A self-confirmed, life-long bachelor, Art Labrum spent his life buried in a book. Socially awkward, with a ruler-straight part in his oiled hair, he reminded Peyton of George McFly from the movie *Back to the Future*. Mr. Labrum's eccentricities made him an easy target for the meaner kids in high school, but Peyton had always liked him. She found his quirks endearing, and he was kind and helpful to his students.

"You know, Peyton, I had a feeling you and Carter would end up together the first time I caught you locking lips in the supply cabinet." He wagged a finger, a smile creeping over his lips.

Peyton chuckled. "Yeah, you weren't too happy about that. Made us do two rounds of detention, if I remember correctly."

He snorted. "Oh, the foibles of youth. To be—" He stopped mid-sentence, looking thoughtful. "You know, the two of you remind me a little of Mr. Darcy and Elizabeth Bennett. You have my sincerest congratulations. It's not often that people have the fortitude to defy convention and follow their hearts."

"There she is ... the lady of the hour," a female voice squealed.

Peyton turned to see two girls about her age approaching.

"How sweet you look tonight," the pretty blonde bubbled. Her dress was poured on—so tight Peyton doubted she could sit down.

"I'm sorry. Do we know each other?"

The girl touched Peyton's arm. "I'm Claire and this is Mindy."

Mr. Labrum shrank into himself. "Well, I must be going," he said in a formal tone. He gave Peyton a slight bow before shuffling away.

Peyton turned her attention to the two girls, her mood dampening slightly. She'd rather endure Mr. Labrum's long quotes a hundred times over than be forced into making small talk with strangers. Then again, maybe she was missing out on a friendship. They were part of Carter's world, and she was about to marry into it. She'd better start developing her own contacts. "It's nice to meet you," she said, in a voice that sounded falsely cheerful to her own ears. "Are you friends of Carter's?"

Claire smirked. "You could say that. Carter and I used to date."

Peyton tensed. "Really? He never mentioned you."

An easy laugh escaped Claire's lips. "You know how Carter is. He probably didn't want to upset you." She waved a hand. "Anyway, it was a thousand years ago. Water under the bridge."

Peyton lifted an eyebrow. And yet she chose to mention it now. *Interesting.*

3

"You're so lucky," Claire chirped, turning to Mindy. "Doesn't she look darling?" She zeroed in on Peyton. "I'll bet you look good in any old thing. I saw your same dress on the clearance rack at Dillard's last season. Only a short girl like you could pull off wearing it. I had to have something specially made by my designer to fit my tiny waist."

Mindy sniggered while Claire fluffed her curls, her lips forming a sultry pout. "I always wondered what kind of girl had enough torque to lasso Carter Webster." She looked Peyton up and down. "Huh," she mused softly. "Just goes to show, you never can tell what's going to make love click."

Mindy giggled and lurched forward. "Funny!" she gasped, wiping at her eyes.

Peyton's cheeks warmed. *All right—I'm done playing nice.* She looked Claire in the eye and smiled brightly as if she were in a toothpaste commercial. "And sometimes, dresses are like clunker cars—no matter how much money you pour into them, they'll never be a classic."

Claire's face turned scarlet like she might have a heat stroke.

Peyton was about to excuse herself when strong arms encircled her waist from behind. She looked back as Carter leaned in, tickling her ear with his warm breath.

"Hey, I've been looking for you. We're about ready to do the toast."

"Oh, I've just been getting acquainted with your old girlfriend."

He jerked. "My what?"

Peyton motioned. "Claire. According to her, the two of you were thick as thieves."

Carter's eyes went large, and Claire suddenly took interest in someone across the way as she caught hold of Mindy's arm. "Oh, look, there's Steven." With a sniff, she cut her eyes at Peyton and Carter. "Well, it was great to see you both. Congratulations again," she quipped, as she and Mindy scattered.

Peyton chuckled dryly. "Yeah, just as I thought."

Carter shook his head, amusement twinkling in his gray eyes. "Peyton," he hummed in a low tone, "what've you been up to?"

She laughed. "She started it."

He pulled her close, gazing into her eyes. "I have no doubt. Poor Claire got more than she bargained for when she tangled with you."

The corners of her lips turned down. "Poor Claire, my eye!" She spiked an eyebrow. "So you did date her?"

"We might've gone out once or twice." A devilish glint lit his eyes. "Not jealous, are you?"

She scowled. "Hardly."

"Don't worry. I only have eyes for you." He leaned in, his voice going husky. "You are so beautiful. I can't wait to get you to myself."

She laughed, a tingle of anticipation circling down her spine. "The minute we say *I do*, I'm all yours."

"I'm counting on it." Carter pulled her closer, swaying to the beat of the music, his eyes locking with hers. "I love you, Peyton Kelly. I always have, and I always will."

"I love you too." Peyton felt her heart swell to the point of exploding. She'd never been this happy. He was so handsome she could hardly breathe when running her fingers through his thick mane of dark blond hair. She loved his strong jaw, with just enough stubble to give him a rough-and-tumble charm, and his kind eyes lit up and flowed warmth when he smiled. He was smart, attentive, witty, and— miracle of miracles—he loved her!

"Ladies and gentlemen, I'd like to make a toast."

Peyton and Carter looked toward the portable stage where Carter's mother, Kathryn, stood, looking regal in a sleek black dress, hair twisted in a chignon. She held a glass of wine in one hand and a microphone in the other.

A waiter offered Peyton and Carter a glass. Peyton was about to decline when Carter whispered in her ear, "It's sparkling water." He winked. "I got your back." Carter knew how much Peyton detested alcohol on account of her alcoholic stepfather.

"Thank you," she mouthed.

"I so appreciate all of you joining us this evening to celebrate the union of my son Carter and the lovely Peyton Kelly." Kathryn paused as if collecting her thoughts. "I'm not ashamed to admit that at first I wasn't sure how Carter and Peyton's relationship would work."

5

Peyton stiffened, not sure where this was going. She saw Carter's jaw clench and his arm tightened protectively around her waist.

A magnanimous smile stretched over Kathryn's lips. "But seeing them together, it's obvious the two of you love each other very much." Her eyes went misty. "And I suppose that's what it's all about—true love." She lifted her glass. "May you have a lifetime of happiness and joy."

Applause broke out around them. "Speech!" a man bellowed from behind.

"Speech!" another man repeated, and then the crowd started chanting it.

Carter held up a hand to quiet the crowd. "Okay, a speech it is." He clasped Peyton's hand and pulled her to the stage, where Kathryn handed him the microphone.

Carter peered over the crowd. "Is someone here getting married?" he asked dubiously, eliciting ripples of laughter.

Peyton gave him a playful shove.

"Seriously, I'm the luckiest man alive. Tomorrow, I'm marrying the woman of my dreams." His voice caught as he turned to Peyton, sincerity shining in his gray eyes. "Thank you for taking a chance on me. I promise I won't let you down."

Peyton's eyes teared up as she nodded.

Carter handed Peyton the microphone. "Your turn."

A commotion went through the crowd. Peyton looked toward the back to see what was happening. Her heart lurched when she saw Harold, her stepfather, staggering through the guests. He mumbled incoherently and pointed toward the stage.

For a second, Peyton was paralyzed with humiliation. Her fairy-tale evening had suddenly turned into a nightmare as she thrust the microphone at Carter and rushed down the steps of the stage to Harold's side. The crowd parted, equal looks of horror and disgust carpeting her way.

"What're you doing?" she seethed. "You need to leave!"

Check and *courtyard* were the only two words Peyton could make out of his garbled speech. She tried to take his arm, but he jerked out of her grasp. Pushing her away, he sent her sprawling backwards, where she landed on her rear end, her beautiful mango dress bunched around her legs.

"Hey!" Carter jumped off the stage and put Harold in a chokehold. Harold tried to resist, but his efforts were futile. Two security guards ran in, took Harold from Carter, and dragged him off the grounds.

"Are you all right?" Carter asked, helping Peyton to her feet.

Tears stung her eyes as she nodded. The twinkling lights, so romantic earlier, now blared. The place was spinning, menacing faces closing in around her. She caught sight of Claire and Mindy's triumphant sneers. Peyton could only imagine what they must be thinking. "I need to go to the bathroom," she hiccupped.

Carter took her arm. "Okay, I'll go with you."

The overseer of the wineries, a silver-haired man with hard eyes, stepped up to Carter. "I'm sorry to interrupt, but can I talk to you for a moment …" He lowered his voice. "About the incident."

Carter looked like he might protest until Peyton put a hand on his arm. "It's okay," she said quickly. "I'll be right back." She needed a little space to pull herself together.

Carter searched her face. "You sure?"

She offered a tight smile. "Yeah."

"Okay," Carter said reluctantly. "I'll be right here."

PEYTON ATTEMPTED to go to the guest bathroom off the foyer, but it was occupied. A maid directed her to another, more private bathroom in the back section of the mansion.

After Peyton composed herself, she had to fight the temptation to head home. Instinctively, she knew if she didn't go back out and show her face tonight, she'd never be able to look these people in the eye again. There'd never been any love lost between Peyton and Harold, even though she'd never outright hated him. But at this moment, she did.

And she was super ticked at her mother. Her mom refused to come to tonight's party because she detested Kathryn Webster. The last Peyton heard, Harold was staying home, too. Why did he have to pick tonight, of all nights, to show up here? Had Peyton's mother come to the party, she might've been able to keep Harold in check before he made a buffoon of himself.

When Peyton left the bathroom, she heard voices coming from the nearby study. She almost walked on by when she heard her name. She halted in her tracks, easing toward the door.

Carter was sitting in the overstuffed chair, his back towards Peyton. Kathryn was standing over him, her expression livid. A catering cart was parked just outside the double French doors, preventing Peyton from getting closer. She attempted to push it aside, but it wouldn't budge. Peyton craned her neck to see inside, without being seen.

Kathryn's voice was harsh, her face pinched. "I've never been so humiliated in my entire life. I told you, it's never going to work with Peyton. She's not like us. You come from two different worlds. I know you feel obligated to her." She held up a finger. "Don't try to deny it, because I can see it in your eyes. That's the problem with you, Carter: you're too good-hearted. You feel sorry for Peyton, but this can't continue. Otherwise, you'll end up resenting her in the end."

Heat stung Peyton's face as she waited for Carter to respond.

What Peyton saw and heard next would be branded in her mind forever as her world shattered to pieces. A tremor started in her hands and rippled through her body. Tears sprang to her eyes as she gulped down a sob and ran the other direction. Her only thought was to get as far away from Carter Webster as possible.

CHAPTER 1

*P*eyton perched her hands on her hips, critically studying the dilapidated farmhouse. It had probably been a showpiece in its day, but time had gotten the upper hand. The relentless Texas heat had boiled off a majority of the paint, leaving the aged wood naked and exposed. The windows were broken, and the front porch was pulling away from the house.

Even though the house had seen better days, the bones were good. And it helped that the property backed up to a high-dollar subdivision. "What year was she built?" Peyton asked, taking hold of the loose handrail as she gingerly walked up the front steps. The wooden planks creaked ominously with every step of her high-heeled boots.

"1945," Trevor said.

"It's got loads of potential … at least on the outside." Houses needing this much work in exclusive areas were hard to come by. Most of them were snapped up before ever going on the market. And ninety-nine percent of the time, a builder would simply bulldoze the old house and build a new one in its place. "Wow. The Brookshires must've pulled a few strings to get this baby."

"It certainly seems that way," Trevor said. "And it gets even better. They're using this house as a weekend getaway."

"Ah, very nice. We're gonna have fun renovating this one." Peyton lifted an eyebrow and gave her business partner a quick grin.

Peyton and Trevor had met when she moved to Ft. Worth. She'd moved to the area, hardly a penny to her name, looking for work in her field—design. Before coming to Ft. Worth, she'd worked as an apprentice under an interior designer at a firm in Healdsburg, California.

In Texas, Peyton got hired at a small design center. Before long, she was doing projects on a freelance basis where she found herself in high demand. After a year, she bought her first fixer-upper and needed an expert to repair the foundation. Trevor came highly recommended through one of her design clients. Not only was Trevor a skilled craftsman, but he was also charming with his quick smile and boyish good looks. The two of them had become fast friends. They started out by partnering together on projects—Peyton overseeing the design and Trevor the construction—and soon developed a solid reputation for reputable work. When Trevor insisted on making a video of one of their renovations, Peyton reluctantly went along with the idea, thinking nothing would come of it. Trevor posted it on YouTube, and their big break came when HGTV called, offering them a show named *Fix It Up*. The Brookshires' home rounded out season one, and negotiations were underway for season two. According to Trevor, they were poised to become the next Chip and Joanna Gaines. Peyton didn't want to point out that there were several differences between her and Trevor and Chip and Joanna, the most noticeable being that Chip and Joanna were married.

Peyton knew Trevor wanted to be more than friends, but she wasn't ready for that. Because they were constantly in the public eye, rumors were always circulating about their supposed secret, behind-the-scenes relationship. Peyton had been tempted to go on the record, stating that she and Trevor were only friends. But their publicist insisted the speculation was good for the ratings. Peyton didn't care what the public thought, but she didn't want to give Trevor any false hope. Carter Webster had drilled a hole the size of Texas straight through the center of her heart. Just thinking about it made her blood boil! Maybe someday, when her anger at him subsided, she would finally be able to open her heart to someone else. Eventually, she wanted to get married and have a family. But for now, she was happy with her life the way it was.

"Let's see what we've got to work with." Trevor opened the door to the house and let her go in first.

The stench of something rotten hit her full force. "Ew!" Peyton cupped a hand over her nose and mouth. "It smells like something crawled in here and died."

He chuckled dryly. "Something probably did."

The entrance was a small room with wooden floors that had gaps so large she could see the ground underneath. Ragged strips were the only thing left of what were once curtains. A narrow staircase led up to the second floor. Globs of plaster were splattered on the floor, giving the impression that someone had attempted to fix the fist-sized holes in the sheetrock and had gotten more plaster on the floor than on the walls.

The initial walkthrough was Peyton's favorite part of a project. And she and Trevor made a practice of doing it away from the cameras so they could talk about it openly and get better prepared for staging a walkthrough with the cameras.

After they'd done a thorough inspection of the downstairs, Trevor turned to her. "What do you think?"

She put a finger to her lips, her mind reeling with possibilities. "We can knock out the wall between the living room and kitchen. Make it one large open space. Rebuild the entire kitchen and paint everything white, with black accents. I love that old farm table in the kitchen. I'd like to rework it into an island." Peyton was a firm believer in salvaging as much of the original edifice as possible. There was something rewarding about seeing potential, whereas others could only see ruin.

"Good idea."

She motioned. "It's too bad the floor has these gaps."

"Yeah, I was thinking the same thing. It'll have to be ripped out. I'd like to replace it with wood flooring though, rather than laminate."

"Agreed."

Trevor pointed to the staircase. "I guess I'd better check out the upstairs."

Peyton made a face. "You won't get me on that staircase. Maybe you should go out to your truck and bring in the ladder."

"Nah." Trevor quirked an adventurous grin and began walking cautiously up the stairs. When he realized the bottom few steps were stable, he bounded up the rest.

"I don't think that's a good idea," she called after him. "Termites holding hands is what that is," she muttered.

A couple of minutes later, she heard Trevor stomping on the floor to check the integrity of the framing. She heard a pop, then looked up as flakes of plaster fell from the ceiling. "Stop!" she yelled. But Trevor continued, making it worse.

An entire section gave way and would have landed square on her head, had she not jumped back. She was just about to make a hasty exit from the room when a plume of dust and dirt mushroomed over her.

Peyton waved her arms, coughing and gagging as she attempted to clear the grit from her mouth. "Hey!" she belted as loud as he could.

The stomping ceased. "Did you say something?" Trevor yelled.

She rolled her eyes. "You're getting plaster all over me!"

He came back downstairs a couple of minutes later. When he saw her appearance, he started laughing.

She narrowed her eyes, trying to brush off the plaster. "It's not funny," she huffed, but couldn't stop the smile from stretching over her lips.

They heard a loud crack, and then large sections of plaster started falling. A minute later, the whole ceiling started to give way. Peyton squealed as a piece landed on her boot.

Trevor grabbed her hand. "Come on, before this place falls on top of us!"

By the time they'd made their escape to the front porch, they were covered from head to toe with dust. They stood there, speechless, looking at one another, until a smile stole over Trevor's lips. "You look ridiculous."

Her eyes widened. "You're one to talk."

Trevor rocked back, and then he started laughing. No longer able to contain her laughter, Peyton joined in. A minute later, they were both doubled over.

Finally, Trevor stood, wiping at his eyes. "You should've seen your face when the ceiling caved in."

"Well, duh! How else was I supposed to react? I thought the whole house was gonna fall down around us. Like Indiana Jones and the Temple of Doom."

"Too bad the camera crew wasn't here. That would've made a great TV segment."

She wagged a finger. "Don't get any ideas. I'm not recreating that scene." Her phone began to vibrate. She retrieved it from her back pocket and frowned. It was her stepsister, Andrea, Harold's daughter. They'd hardly spoken since Peyton left California; she couldn't image why Andrea would be calling now. Strange.

"Hello?" she said hesitantly.

"Peyton, this is Andrea."

"Hey."

Silence.

Irritation flickered over Peyton. "Andrea, are you there? What's going on?"

A sob came over the phone. "It's Dad … and your mom. They're dead!"

Peyton gasped, the air leaving her lungs. "What?"

"T-they died in a car accident."

The words seemed to be coming from far away as Peyton's knees buckled.

CHAPTER 2

Funny how death could make Peyton do the one thing she swore up and down she wasn't ready to do—return home. When she had moved to Texas, she vowed she would make a success of herself before ever coming back. And by many accounts, she'd accomplished everything she'd set out to do. Even though she still wasn't ready to face the past, here she was.

Of course, Peyton had no way of knowing her mom's life would be taken, and that she would end up inheriting half of the circa 1901 Queen Anne Victorian Home that'd been in her family for three generations—the Kelly Bed & Breakfast.

Technically, it had never been a bed and breakfast in Peyton's lifetime, but that was what the home was originally built to be. All throughout Peyton's growing-up years, her mom, Rosemary, had grand plans to turn it into an operating bed and breakfast again, but she was never able to make any progress. It was really only something she talked about—a dream to hold on to when times grew hard.

The place looked smaller than Peyton remembered ... and shabbier. The yard was grossly overgrown and littered with junk. An old car sat next to the garage. Beside it, a rusted washing machine lay on its side, choked with weeds. And if that wasn't bad enough, it didn't help that the body of the house was a screaming Pepto-Bismol pink with baby blue accents. Rosemary had selected the colors, insisting that she wanted the bed and breakfast to resemble the Painted Ladies in San Francisco. The selection was so awful, Peyton wondered if she'd chosen the colors just to annoy Kathryn Webster. It would've been just like her mother to do something nonsensical like that. There'd never been any warm fuzzies between Rosemary and Kathryn, but things had gotten a thousand times worse when Peyton and Carter got engaged.

For as long as Peyton could remember, Kathryn had been trying to buy the old home, but Rosemary wouldn't entertain any of her offers, insisting she'd rather live in squalor and keep her home intact than sell it to Kathryn, who'd bulldoze it like it never existed.

Peyton looked past the old homestead to the sloping vineyard in the distance and the enormous mansion and winery that sat prominently on the hill overlooking the valley. She could only imagine how irked Kathryn must be to have this shabby house marring her view.

She couldn't look at the mansion without thinking of Carter. An unexpected pang of sadness went through her. Did Carter know she was back in town? She hadn't heard a word from him since her return. He hadn't even bothered to show up for her mother and stepfather's funeral. She scowled. *Typical.* Then again, maybe it was for the best. Seeing him again would only unearth a world of heartache.

She'd come back for the funeral, but then returned to Texas and the renovation on the Brookshire's home. It had taken her two long months to wrap up that project and get back here. Despite misgivings about facing ghosts of the past, the comfort of home settled around her like a familiar blanket. She'd forgotten how incredibly beautiful the Sonoma Valley was in the fall. The air tasted of crisp apples, and the trees were ablaze with lusty red and yellow leaves. Clusters of plump, ripe grapes dotted the vineyards. Harvest time, or "crush" as the locals called it, was only a week away.

As Peyton glanced at the B&B, she had the impression the wise old windows were staring into her very soul, seeing through her carefully crafted exterior to the naïve, vulnerable girl she once was. She'd felt so insignificant and lacking, growing up here in this run-down house with her eccentric mother and alcoholic stepfather. Especially compared to Carter's sophisticated world.

And now? Now she wasn't sure. She'd come a long way in Texas, but was it enough? *What will you do with the knowledge you've gained?* the house seemed to ask. Normally, she was able to maintain a degree of separation between herself and the houses she fixed up, helping her view the project professionally. But there was little hope of remaining objective about this house, which is why she rejected her publicist's suggestion to make the renovation of her family home the kick-off for season two of the show. She needed to deal with this on her own terms, away from the cameras.

She could almost hear her mother's laughter, remembering how they baked brownies and sang at the top of their lungs to the merry tunes playing on the radio. Those were the memories she wanted to hold on to—not the images of her stepfather Harold coming home drunk in the middle of the night. Or, how Peyton would lay huddled in bed, her ears covered with a pillow to drown out the cursing and screaming from her mom and Harold that continued until the early hours of the morning. Rosemary believed she could change Harold, but that had been her fatal mistake. Harold was drunk when he ran their vehicle into a ravine, killing them both instantly. She exhaled, trying to push away the gloomy thoughts.

As Peyton walked up the front steps, Trevor emerged from the door. "There you are. I've been looking all over for you." He stopped. "Are you okay? You have a strange look on your face."

"Yeah, it's just a lot to take in." She offered a strained smile. "I keep expecting to see my mom at every turn. This place was such a part of her. I still can't believe she's gone." Her eyes misted, and she blinked to stay the tears.

Trevor placed a hand on her arm. "I'm sorry."

She nodded. "Thanks. I really appreciate you dropping everything and coming here to assess the house. You're a good friend."

"Of course."

Peyton could tell from the way Trevor's eyebrows knit together that he didn't like the reference to the word *friend*. She felt a guilty twinge for asking Trevor to come here. On the one hand, she didn't want to give him false hope that they would ever be anything more than friends. On the other hand, she really did need his help—both with the house and for emotional support. Trevor was her closest friend, but she knew they couldn't go on like this forever. Sooner or later, she would have to either open up that part of herself to him or cut him loose. But, she had enough on her plate right now without worrying about that. Luckily, before it got too awkward, Trevor changed the subject.

"Those hairline cracks in the wall of the back bedroom on the first floor make me nervous."

"The house is over a hundred years old. Maybe it's just settling."

"Yeah … that's possible. But it could also mean there are structural weaknesses in the foundation. Only one way to know for sure. I'm headed to the crawlspace to check it out." He motioned with his head. "Wanna come?"

"No … sorry. Andrea was supposed to be here at ten." She glanced at her cell phone. It was now ten-thirty. Punctuality was not high on her stepsister's priority list.

After Trevor disappeared into the crawlspace, Peyton went back into the house to wait. She'd almost given up on Andrea when she heard the hum of a car engine. She drew aside the lace curtains to see a new Range Rover pull into the driveway. Her brows scrunched when Andrea opened the door and got out. A Rover was an expensive vehicle for a high school teacher's salary.

Peyton and Andrea had spoken as few words as possible to one another during the funeral. Then, they'd become co-owners of the house. As soon as Peyton realized that was the case, she tried to reach out to Andrea so they could at least have a conversation. But Andrea hadn't answered her calls or texts. She was about to give up hope of ever communicating with Andrea when she received a text from her. It was short and to the point, saying she would stop by the house today.

Peyton steeled herself for the confrontation sure to take place.

There was no way she and Andrea could work together to restore this place. Andrea hated everything about it, whereas for Peyton, it was the only link she had to her mother and ancestors. She still couldn't understand why her mother felt the need to leave half of everything to Andrea. Then again, she'd probably done it to appease Harold. Rosemary spent the bulk of Peyton's growing-up years walking on eggshells around the man, trying to pretend they were one big, happy family. In reality, they'd been anything but.

The only option was to buy Andrea out. Peyton had enough money in savings to offer her a sizeable down payment. She could pay the rest in installments so she wouldn't exhaust her cash. Surely Andrea would go for that. She wouldn't have any use for this old house, and money talked.

As she watched Andrea strut to the door, Peyton was struck by how opposite the two of them were, even in looks. Andrea was fair with a thin face, blonde hair, and long legs, whereas Peyton was olive toned and petite, with dark hair and brown eyes. A Cameron Diaz meets Jennifer Lopez scenario. Peyton's real dad was Latino—a migrant worker who'd come to work a season in the vineyards. Her mother had fallen madly in love with him, but he wasn't ready to settle down. He'd moved on to another place by the time Peyton was born. Peyton had only seen a couple of pictures of him but could definitely see a resemblance, except that she had lighter skin with her mom's high cheekbones and defined features.

Peyton and Andrea were in their early teens when their parents married. At first, the two girls merely tolerated each other, both doing their best to adjust to this new life and the instant family they'd suddenly been thrown into. They might've eventually been able to find some common ground had Carter Webster not stepped into the picture. Andrea had a crush on Carter, even though she hardly knew him. When Peyton and Carter started dating, the situation between the stepsisters escalated to a bitter rivalry that continued to this day.

Andrea opened the door and strolled in without knocking. Peyton's first inclination was to say something about manners, but she thought better of it. Andrea was an equal owner, with as much right to be here as Peyton. And Peyton wanted to resolve the matter as amicably as possible. "Thanks for coming."

"Sure," Andrea sniffed.

They walked into the front parlor.

Peyton motioned. "Have a seat."

Andrea looked disdainfully at the battered loveseat. For a second, Peyton thought she might refuse. But she finally plopped down, a sour expression marring her face as she made a flourish with her hand, encompassing the room. "This place is a dump. Always has been. Always will be." She placed her purse beside her and crossed her legs. Her skirt was so short that Peyton had to quickly avert her eyes to spare herself a glimpse of undies.

Peyton scooted to the edge of her seat and wet her lips nervously. "The house does need a lot of work. That's what I wanted to talk to you about."

Andrea reached in her purse and pulled out a compact and tube of lipstick. "So talk," she said, uncapping the lipstick and sliding it over her lips.

Tension crawled up Peyton's neck. The lipstick ploy was Andrea's way of letting her know she wasn't worthy of her full attention. "I want to buy your half of the property."

Andrea traced the corners of her lips with the tip of her pinky finger to smooth out the lipstick before snapping the compact shut. "Sorry, no can do."

Peyton's collar grew tight around her neck. It was just like Andrea to make this difficult. "You hate this place. You always have. I can pay you a sizeable amount of money up front and payments every month. It's a good deal," she finished, not trying to keep the irritation out of her voice.

Andrea uncrossed her legs as she dropped the compact and lipstick back into her purse and slung the strap over her shoulder as she stood. She fluffed her hair and pursed her lips. "I've already sold my half to someone else."

Peyton's heart dropped. "What?"

Andrea walked across the floor towards the door.

Peyton followed close on her heels. "Why didn't you tell me?"

Andrea held up a hand, not even bothering to turn around. "I'm telling you now."

Peyton felt the room spin. "Who did you sell it to?"

Andrea opened the door. "I'm not at liberty to say. But don't worry, you'll find out soon enough." Her cold eyes flickered over Peyton as she flashed a false smile. "Well, I guess this is goodbye. Have a good life."

A futile anger sparked over Peyton, and she had the urge to slap the smug expression off Andrea's face. Thankfully, before she gave in to the temptation, Trevor came up the front steps.

"So this is the stepsister I've heard so much about." He held out his hand. "Howdy. I'm Trevor Spencer."

Rather than shaking his hand, Andrea gave him the once-over, her eyes settling on his boots. "Well, yes you are," she quipped.

Trevor's hand hung awkwardly in the air before he dropped it to his side.

"You look just as good in person as you do on TV," Andrea said, flipping the ends of her hair. She glanced back at Peyton. "I see you've traded the rich boy for the cowboy." She let out a sarcastic chuckle. "Same old Peyton. Can't get through the day without a man on your arm."

The corners of Trevor's lips went down, and he looked like he was going to say something, but before he could get a word out, Andrea was already to her SUV. She started the engine and sped off.

Trevor scowled. "Who peed in her Cheerios?"

"I did … unfortunately." If Peyton had it to do over again, she would hand Carter to Andrea on a silver platter and save herself the heartache.

He grimaced. "She's just as awful as you described."

Frustration boiled inside Peyton. "Yep, and she's gonna make me pay dearly for every injustice she can dream up. I should've seen this coming."

"What?"

LOVE UNDER FIRE

Tears sprang to Peyton's eyes, and she blinked them back. "She sold her half of the house to someone else."

The horrified look on Trevor's face mirrored her feelings, making the situation even worse. "Can she do that?" he asked.

Peyton threw her hands in the air. "She did!" The whole thing was absurd. The anger that raged inside her was so fierce it made her shake. How could her mother have been stupid enough to leave Andrea half of this place? Shackling herself to Harold all of those years was bad enough, but this was inexcusable. She placed her thumb and index finger on the bridge of her nose, pinching each side to stay the dull headache that formed.

Trevor stepped up to her and began rubbing her arms. "It's gonna be okay."

A lump grew in her throat. "I don't know that it will."

"Who did she sell to?"

A harsh laugh escaped Peyton's throat. "She didn't even have the decency to tell me." All the despair and hurt she'd felt over the past two months came to a head, and she couldn't hold back the tears. She hated Andrea for being so mean and spiteful, but most of all she hated Harold for taking her mother away.

Trevor put his arms around her and let her cry.

The sound of an approaching car caused Peyton to jerk away from him. Was it Andrea? A hot anger seared through her as she lifted her head from Trevor's chest to look. But instead of Andrea's Rover, a black Lamborghini pulled into the driveway. Hastily, she stepped away from Trevor and wiped at her tears.

Trevor let out a low whistle. "Nice ride."

A moment later, Carter Webster strode up the steps, and Peyton found herself staring into the very face she'd spent the last few years trying to forget.

"Forgive me for interrupting," Carter said, his smoky eyes lingering on Peyton's arm long enough for her to realize Trevor still had a hand on her. Self-consciously, she stepped back and cleared her throat. Of all the times for her to lose it! Fate must be having a heyday with this one. She'd gone through a thousand scenarios in her mind

21

about how she would react when she came face to face with Carter, and melting into a puddle of tears was not one of them. She straightened her shoulders, trying to reclaim what little shred of dignity she could.

"Carter, what're you doing here?"

Carter's eyes held hers, and she felt the blood throbbing in her temples. Her face felt flush, her legs unsteady. So much for remaining unaffected by Carter Webster! A thousand memories assaulted her as all the little pep talks she'd had with herself vanished like smoke into the crisp fall air.

Carter was still as handsome as always, with his wavy, dark blond hair, even features, and angular jaw covered in a short layer of sexy stubble. But there were faint creases around his eyes, and he seemed harder around the edges—the experiences of life crowding out the softness of youth. The Carter she remembered had been uncomfortable with his excessive wealth and never quite sure of himself. But looking at him now, with his confident demeanor, trendy clothes, and flashy sports car, she got the impression he'd settled into his status, finally becoming the man his mother had always wanted him to be. Resentment pricked up the back of her neck.

"Hardly the way I would expect you to greet an old friend," Carter said.

"Is that what we are?"

He arched an eyebrow, faint amusement lighting his eyes. "You tell me."

Her heart lurched as she moistened her lips, frantically searching for a way to answer him.

As always, Trevor came to her aid, stepping up and extending his hand. "I'm Trevor Spencer, Peyton's business partner."

Carter's eyes flashed with something indistinguishable. "I'm Carter, her ex-fiancé."

Guilt pummeled over Peyton when she heard Trevor's slight intake of breath. She'd never told him about Carter; only that she'd been involved in a relationship before coming to Texas.

Trevor clasped Carter's hand. "It's nice to meet you."

"Likewise. I watch your show."

Peyton was surprised. It had never entered her mind that Carter would watch her show. Suddenly, she felt exposed. An awkward moment passed before Trevor spoke.

"If y'all will excuse me, I need to finish up in the crawlspace." He squeezed Peyton's arm, giving her a look that said, *Let me know if you need me, and I'll come running.* He offered Carter a curt nod before going down the steps.

Carter cocked his head. "Seems like a nice enough guy."

"Yeah." She ran a hand through her hair. The last thing she wanted to do was discuss Trevor with Carter.

Carter motioned. "Aren't you going to invite me in?"

She folded her arms over her chest, studying him. "I haven't decided yet."

He chuckled lightly, leaning into her personal space. Her pulse bumped up a notch when he touched her hair.

She jerked back, her eyes going wide. "What're you doing?"

He held up his fingers. "You had something in your hair."

"Oh ... thanks," she mumbled. One whiff of his spicy cologne was all it took to unleash a flood of memories. How many times had they stood in this very spot? Holding each other, promising their undying love—believing the world wasn't big enough to hold their dreams. She'd been so intoxicated with Carter that he'd consumed her every thought.

She realized with a jolt that Carter was studying her. Was he experiencing those same memories? She cleared the cobwebs from her head. There was no way she was falling back into Carter's trap. She'd fought too hard to stand on her own. She couldn't ... wouldn't revert back to that fragile girl she'd been.

"Do you mind if we go inside? There are a few things we need to discuss."

She planted her feet on the porch. "Really? What things?"

A crease appeared between his brows. "Same old Peyton, always questioning everything."

She bristled. "Same old Carter, always being obscure. Maybe you should just tell me whatever you have to say."

He shifted his feet. "Well, for starters, I'm sorry about your mother."

The omission of her stepfather spoke volumes, a reminder of how well he knew her. "Thanks."

"And I'm sorry I wasn't able to attend the funeral."

"No big deal. I didn't realize you weren't there."

He looked surprised and a little hurt.

Her first impulse was to say something to ease his discomfort. *Old habits die hard.* She forced a smile. "It was nice of you to stop by to offer your condolences." Being in such close proximity to Carter was draining. She needed space to regain her composure. "If you'll excuse me, I have a lot of work to do."

"Yeah … about that … you know, I could really use a drink of water. I just drove back from San Francisco, and I'm parched."

She rolled her eyes. "Seriously?" She cut her eyes toward his house. "It's not like you have far to go." She put a hand on her hip, studying him. "Carter, why are you really here?"

He held up a finger. "One glass of water, and I'll tell you." A ghost of a smile touched his lips. "You wouldn't deny a thirsty man that, would you?"

She sighed. "Fine. Come on."

As he followed her to the kitchen, Peyton couldn't help but wonder what Carter must think of the shabby surroundings. As a teenager, she'd been ashamed of the condition of her home, especially since Carter came from such wealth. The insecurities from her childhood came rushing back, and for a split second, she felt like a kid again.

No. You are a successful designer with your own TV show. You have nothing to prove to anyone, especially not Carter Webster.

She opened the fridge, reached for a water pitcher, and poured him a glass.

He drained it, then placed it on the counter. "Thanks."

She nodded, waiting for him to speak.

He took a deep breath, a troubled expression coming over him. "As I said earlier, I came to offer my condolences ... and to look over my property." He looked around the kitchen.

"What do you mean?"

His eyes met hers. "This place."

Her blood ran cold. "You bought Andrea's half."

"Yep."

She had the hysterical urge to laugh ... or cry. *This can't be happening. Please let it be a nightmare. Let me wake up.* Somehow, she managed to find her voice. "What do you want?"

Carter poured himself another glass of water and took a long drink. Peyton watched his Adam's apple go up and down as he swallowed.

"I can buy you out."

He lowered the glass. "Or I could buy you out. I'll pay top dollar. And that's saying a lot for this broken-down place."

Of all the arrogant things to say! Carter had turned into his mother, assuming money could buy anything. But it couldn't buy her. "So you can tear down the house that's been in my family for three generations?" She squared her jaw. "I don't think so."

"Be reasonable, Peyton. Your life's not here anymore. You have your fancy show and your boyfriend. You don't belong here."

The cutting words hit their mark as fury spiked through her, making her feel like her head would explode. "How dare you tell me where I do and don't belong. This place is my home. And I'll not let you nor anyone else dictate what's gonna happen to it!"

A hard amusement glittered in his eyes. "But you're forgetting. Half of it belongs to me. I can and I will determine what happens to this place." He looked around, disgust plain on his face. "It's falling apart."

"Get out!"

He rocked back, his eyes going hard. "No."

"What?"

He leaned back against the counter and crossed his arms over his chest. "I have just as much right to be here as you. And I'm not leaving until I get darn good and ready."

All reason flew out the window as Peyton turned on the faucet and reached for the sprayer. Shock registered on Carter's features the instant before she sprayed him in the face. "I said *get out*. Get off my property!"

He held up his hands and ducked his head. "Stop. Peyton."

A sense of power rushed over her as she laughed maniacally. "Not so tough now, are ya?"

Carter bolted forward and attempted to wrench the sprayer out of her hands, but she held on tight. He leaned, and the weight of his body sent her toppling backwards. She slipped and went down to the floor, pulling him down on top of her. When she began swatting at him, he pinned her arms to the floor.

"Stop it, Peyton. You're acting crazy."

Rage boiled over her as she tried to wiggle out from underneath him. "Get off me!"

"It doesn't have to be this way. We can handle this like rational adults."

"You come traipsing in here with your snub-the-world attitude, thinking you can tell me what to do with my house. But you can't." Her voice rose to a frenzied height. "Do you hear me? I said you can't!"

"Is there a problem here?"

Peyton looked up to see Trevor standing over them, his fists clenched like he was ready to pounce.

Carter gave Peyton a withering look. "No, there's no problem, I was just leaving." He released Peyton's arms and got to his feet, wiping the water from his face. His eyes cut into Peyton's as his lips became a tight line. "This is not over. We can either come to an agreement or you should find a good attorney. Your decision. I'm done trying to reason with you."

Peyton sat up, rubbing her wrists. "I said get out," she muttered through clenched teeth.

"Gladly." Carter turned on his heel and stormed out.

Trevor just stood there, looking at her.

"What?" she barked, getting to her feet and feeding the sprayer back into its place on the sink. Angrily, she yanked a paper towel from the roll and blotted her face.

"You never told me you were engaged."

"That's because it's a non-issue."

He lifted an eyebrow. "From where I'm standing, I'd say it's an issue. A big one."

CHAPTER 3

*K*athryn's heels clicked on the white marble floor as she walked over to the large windows in the great room. She stared over the neatly lined vineyards spread like a carpet over the rolling hills and sighed. It had been a rough day. The lab tests showed that the spot on her nose was basal cell carcinoma. This was the third time she'd dealt with this cancer. The other two times had been spots on her forehead.

She crossed both arms over her chest, taking in a deep breath. Her doctor explained that the basil cell carcinoma was reoccurring so often because of her weakened immune system. For the past three years, she'd been battling chronic lymphocytic leukemia. When she first found out she had leukemia, she was devastated. But then she realized that CLL was typically a slow-progressing cancer that was termed "chronic" because people lived with it for many years. Two years ago, she'd underdone a round of chemotherapy and had good results. But it had taken a toll on her body. Most of the time, she could manage her symptoms by planning ahead and not getting too worn out or stressed.

Her expression turned sour. "Try to avoid stress," her doctor said. But that was easier said than done. She'd been stressed to the max the past few days, thanks to Peyton Kelly. She glared at the shabby roof of the Kelly place. It was the only thing marring the otherwise pristine landscape—the perpetual pebble in her shoe. Kathryn couldn't believe it when she learned Peyton Kelly was back. When Peyton skipped town on the eve of her wedding to Carter, Kathryn thought she'd gotten rid of the horrid girl for good. And she might have, had Rosemary not gotten herself killed in a stupid car accident. Of all the rotten luck!

At least Rosemary was dense enough to leave half of the home to Andrea. It had been easy to buy her half; now they just had to convince Peyton to sell. But Peyton was contrary, like Rosemary. The only thing they had working in their favor was that Peyton had built a new life in Texas. Maybe the rumors about Peyton being involved with her co-star, Trevor Spencer, were true. There was a chance Peyton had come back to tie up loose ends before going on her way.

Kathryn's desire for the Kelly property was twofold. Yes, she wanted to tear down the eyesore and build a lodge in its place. But she also wanted to make sure Peyton's presence was erased ... for Carter's sake.

Even though Carter swore up and down he was over Peyton, Kathryn knew better. She'd come into the den one evening and caught him watching Peyton's TV show. The anguished look on Carter's face said it all.

There was a time when Kathryn had hoped Carter might follow in his late father's footsteps and go into politics. But Carter made it quite clear he had no intention whatsoever of doing that. So she'd set her sights on grooming him to take over the family business, which consisted of four hundred acres of vineyards, two olive groves, three wineries, two restaurants, a five-star resort, and the palatial Tuscan Villa where Kathryn lived. Kathryn inherited the business from her parents, wealthy investors who'd purchased the then-struggling vineyard in the early seventies and turned it into a thriving business. It was under Kathryn's watch that the two additional wineries, the restaurants, and the resort were added.

As it turned out, Kathryn had quite a head for business, which was ironic considering that when she was in her twenties, her life's ambition was to become a stage actress. Kathryn's parents assumed she would step into the role of leadership as soon as she reached adulthood. They were devastated when she left Sonoma Valley shortly after high school and moved to New York to pursue her dream. She managed to procure a small role in an off Broadway play, which is how she caught Bradley's eye. Bradley was in New York on business. It was Bradley who persuaded Kathryn to move back to her home in Sonoma Valley and take over the vineyard and winery. Kathryn's passion for acting then took a secondary role to the business. Nevertheless, she was still heavily involved with the local theater and often did cameo appearances in its productions.

It was up to Carter to carry on the family tradition and run the family business. Carter would eventually find a wife and settle down. The trick was making sure he found the right wife. A few months ago, she'd orchestrated an introduction to Millicent Harrington, the daughter of a well-connected family in San Francisco. Millicent was beautiful, charming, and easily manipulated. If everything went according to plan, Kathryn would acquire the Kelly property and build another resort in its place. Carter would marry Millicent and give her a few grandchildren. All she had to do was make sure Peyton Kelly didn't get in the way. But she knew that the situation needed to be handled by someone other than her. Maybe Fitz, the overseer for the wineries and resorts? He was so smitten with her that he would jump at the chance to help. But she didn't need a Doberman at this point. This needed to be handled delicately. And she had just the perfect person in mind.

As if he could read her mind, Fitz strode into the room. Around Kathryn's same age, he was a little under six feet tall with silver hair so short his scalp showed through. Fitz was solidly built and physically fit with ropey muscles that stretched across his broad shoulders. His watchful eyes took a careful assessment of her.

"How did it go today?"

"About as well as can be expected. The spot needs to be removed. And I'll need to get a plastic surgeon to avoid scarring." Miraculously, Kathryn had been able to preserve her beauty despite the cancer and chemo. And that was important, because it was primarily her beauty that kept Fitz at her beck and call. Fitz came from an unsavory background and had spent the bulk of his career in the army before finding his place at Webster Wineries. Kathryn suspected that Fitz sometimes used unscrupulous methods to keep everything running smoothly and to make sure the wineries maintained their competitive edge. Fitz was good at his job, and she didn't ask too many questions. That way, she could maintain a state of plausible deniability.

Fitz stepped up behind Kathryn and began rubbing her shoulders. "You're tense."

Kathryn appreciated the feel of Fitz's strong hands as they worked the tension out of her muscles. She was attracted to Fitz's strength and raw ruthlessness; she depended on him for emotional support as well as his prowess in running her businesses. Yet a part of her was also repelled by him. A blunt instrument like Fitz could never fit into her tidy social world.

A noise caught her attention, and she turned to see Carter. She could sense his disapproval as his eyes moved over her and Fitz. As discretely as she could, she moved away from Fitz. "What happened to you? You're soaking wet." She raised a penciled eyebrow. "And dripping water on the floor."

A dark look came over Carter's face. "Peyton. That's what happened to me."

Alarm splattered through Kathryn. "I thought we agreed you weren't going near her."

Carter's gray eyes turned stony as his eyebrows made a sharp V. "Those were your words, Mother. I never agreed to that. But I might as well have. I don't know why I even try," he muttered. "If you'll excuse me, I seem to be in need of a shower."

As Kathryn watched Carter go with a dejected look on his face, poker-hot anger scorched through her. It had taken less than a day for Peyton Kelly to get her claws back into Carter. It was history repeating itself. She had to do something about that girl. Fast!

She realized Fitz was studying her. His eyes held hers as he spoke. "You just say the word, and I'll take care of the girl."

The prospect was so tempting she could almost taste it. One word from her lips ... or even the slightest nod, and Peyton would no longer be a problem. But if Carter found out, he'd never forgive her. "I'll try it my way first. If that doesn't work, we'll consider other options."

~

NORMALLY, Carter prided himself on maintaining a healthy level of self-control in any given situation. Heck, he'd even studied conflict resolution in college. At the Webster entities, he was frequently called upon to resolve personality conflicts between employees. His rational mind knew that when two parties were at odds, the only way to reach a solution was to stay above the fray. But when Peyton sprayed him in the face, something inside him snapped. And now he was feeling the classic effect of what the textbooks termed *cognitive dissonance*—the mental stress that occurred when a person's behavior failed to match up to their belief.

He smiled grimly. It was so cut-and-dry according to the world of academia. But the writers of those books had obviously never met Peyton Kelly. She didn't fit any mold, and she could get under his skin in a way no other woman ever had. She was the spicy jalapeño in an otherwise bland dish of vegetables and broth. He'd wondered how he would feel when he came face to face with her. Seeing Peyton on TV was one thing. But in the flesh, old feelings came rushing back, hurt and betrayal at the top of the list. He still had no idea why she'd skipped town the day before their wedding. There'd been no explanation. Nothing.

Yesterday, as Carter drove back from San Francisco, he'd run a dozen scenarios through his head, pondering over what he would say to Peyton when he saw her. First and foremost, he'd demand to know why she'd left him at the altar. But when he pulled into the driveway and saw her in the arms of Trevor Spencer, he decided he wouldn't give her the satisfaction of knowing how deeply she'd hurt him. It was better to leave the past alone and focus on the future. The Kelly House was the only thing standing in the way of his future resort. He and his mom owned the surrounding land, so acquiring it was only logical. And despite her protests, Peyton couldn't care much about that broken-down place, or she wouldn't have left. Had her mom not died, she'd still be living a charmed life in Texas.

Maybe seeing Peyton today was a good thing. He could finally come to terms with her rejection and move on. He was an eligible bachelor, with a long line of girls who would jump at the chance to date him. But even as he thought the words, an image of Peyton filled his mind. Petite and delicate and yet so explosive. It had been a running joke between them that dynamite came in small packages—as illustrated by their meeting today.

A slight smile touched his lips. It was so Peyton to spray him with water. He loved the light that danced in her almond-shaped eyes when she smiled. And the way her dark, wavy hair cascaded down her back like a sheet of luminescent water. There was a timeless aspect to her finely carved bone structure that reminded him of a Greek statue. Life with Peyton had been exciting and unpredictable. And he loved every minute of it … right up until the moment she left him.

Bitterness rose like acid in his throat. Would he ever be free of Peyton? The problem was that she'd laid the framework of everything he'd come to expect in a woman.

When he was a kid, Peyton was simply the poor girl that lived in the run-down house at the bottom of the hill. She didn't appear on his radar until his freshman year in high school. His mother had wanted him to attend a private school, but his dad insisted it was important for the family to associate with their neighbors and take an active role in the community. Kathryn reluctantly allowed Carter to attend public school, but forbid him to date any of the girls there, especially Peyton Kelly. That was all well and good until the day Carter walked into the cafeteria and saw her. His world tilted, and everything filled with glorious color.

Like most typical ninth-grade boys, he would've preferred to have his head bludgeoned rather than let Peyton know he had a crush on her. So he spent the next few months tormenting her instead. He lost track of the number of times he "accidentally" hit her with the basketball in gym class or shot spitballs in her hair during chemistry. What he didn't count on, however, was Peyton retaliating. She filled his locker with shaving cream and put glue in his tennis shoes. When he tromped over to her house to confront her, she happened to be washing the family car. An argument ensued that ended with Peyton dumping a bucket of soapy water over his head.

Eventually, they called a truce, and Carter found plenty of excuses to keep coming around. They became the best of friends but didn't start dating until their senior year. Even though Carter went off to college at Berkeley, he and Peyton kept in close contact. They got engaged a few months after he graduated. Carter had thought that he was leading a charmed life—marrying the girl of his dream; until everything exploded in his face.

He didn't consciously realize it until today, but a small of part of him had been holding out hope that there might be a chance for him and Peyton to start over. That hope was dashed the minute he saw Peyton in Trevor's arms. Now he had to figure out the best course to take with the house.

His phone buzzed. He pulled it from his pocket and read the text from Millicent Harrington, telling him how thrilled she was to accompany him to crush the following week. The Webster Wineries were famous for their lavish starlight extravaganza held at the mansion each year. It featured the finest food and wine in the valley, along with a live band and dancing.

Carter and Millicent had been dating for a little over six months. Millicent wanted to take things to the next level, but Carter held back, telling himself he wasn't ready to settle down. Millicent was beautiful, charming, smart … and she adored him. A marriage to Millicent would make his mother happy. And Carter wanted to please her, especially considering how fragile she'd become because of the leukemia. With a resolved sigh, he texted Millicent back with a simple …

Looking forward to seeing you this weekend.

He winced when she sent him a book-long response gushing about the important people who were attending the event and what she was going to wear. He scrolled through the text, skimming the majority of it.

Maybe he should invite Peyton to crush—let her see Millicent on his arm. Then she would realize he no longer had the slightest romantic interest in her whatsoever. A smile spread over his lips. Yes, that would help even the score a little.

CHAPTER 4

*I*t had been two days since Peyton's run-in with Carter, and she'd not heard a single word from him. Should she contact an attorney rather than waiting around like a sitting duck for Carter to make his move? Trevor questioned whether they should continue working on the house, since they were uncertain about what the future held. But Peyton insisted on forging ahead. She couldn't stand to be idle and thought it might bode well with a judge if she were already in the process of fixing the place up when they went to court.

Luckily, the foundation was secure, so Peyton and Trevor turned their sights to the interior, starting first in the kitchen. It was in such bad shape, the only option was to gut it and start over. They removed the wall between the kitchen and living room and tore out the old cabinets. By the end of the second day, Peyton was exhausted. Normally, she and Trevor hired construction crews to help with the demolition. But since Peyton was paying for the renovations, they were doing as much as they could themselves to conserve funds. However, at this point, Peyton was starting to think they should've gone ahead and hired people to help. Every muscle in her body ached, and she was covered from head to toe in dirt and grime. She desperately needed a shower and a nap.

She and Trevor were sitting on the front porch, catching their breath, when Trevor turned to her. "What's the story with Carter?"

Peyton wrinkled her nose, her expression souring. "If it's all the same to you, I really don't want to talk about it right now."

"Oh, no, you don't. You've got to be straight with me on this one."

Her lips formed a grim line as she looked at the afternoon sun casting golden rays across the yard and surround vineyards. She did owe him an explanation, especially since he was putting time and effort into a house half-owned by the guy. "Carter and I were high school sweethearts. Our relationship continued when he was in college. When he graduated, we decided it was a good time to get married. Everything was going great ... or so I thought, until the day before our wedding." Her features hardened. "That's when I realized I was making the biggest mistake of my life. So I left. And you know the rest of the story."

"You left the day before your wedding?"

"Yes," she uttered.

He let out a low whistle. "No wonder the man's got a burr in his boot. I'd be mad too."

Peyton's face fell. "You're taking his side?"

Trevor held up a hand. "I'm not taking anybody's side. I just can't imagine someone up and leaving the day before their wedding. Why'd you do it?"

Her face flushed. "I told you, I realized I was making the biggest mistake of my life." She'd not told anyone the things she'd seen and heard that night, and she didn't intend to now. She stood. "Do you want something to drink?"

"So, the topic of Carter's off limits?"

"Yep," she snipped, giving him a firm look.

Trevor let out a breath. "Fine. I'll take a water."

Peyton relaxed, grateful Trevor wasn't pressing her for answers. "How about a nice warm bottle of Perrier? I can't exactly get you cold water, seeing as how we don't have a fridge. I'll get a mini-fridge that we can put in the living room."

"I suppose beggars can't be choosers. Warm Perrier it is."

They looked as a car pulled into the driveway. Peyton tensed. Was this the moment where an attorney served her with papers? Peyton straightened her shoulders as the woman got out and slammed her car door closed. She was almost to the front steps before Peyton recognized her.

"Courtney?"

Courtney waved. "Hey. Long time no see."

"Oh my gosh, it's so good to see you." Peyton bridged the distance between them in two quick steps and embraced Courtney in a tight hug. Then she realized she was covered in sheetrock dust. She pulled back and began wiping Courtney's shoulders. "Sorry."

"No worries. I guess it comes with the territory. I heard you're remodeling the old place."

Peyton cocked her head. "Really? Who told you?"

"Have you been away so long you've forgotten how quickly news travels in Cloverdale?"

"Yeah, maybe I have," Peyton chuckled. "But it's all starting to come back." She took a good look at Courtney. She was thinner than Peyton remembered. Her pixie hair was streaked with blonde, and she was dressed in a tailored black shirt and dress pants—the outfit of a professional woman. "I didn't recognize you at first." She touched Courtney's hair. "You chopped your hair off." When she'd last seen Courtney, her hair was down to her waist.

"Well, it has been years since we've seen each other," Courtney replied tartly. "Had I not seen you on TV, I would've thought you'd dropped off the face of the earth." She turned to Trevor. "It's pretty sad when you have to learn about your best friend through gossip blogs on the Internet."

She and Courtney had been close friends since their junior year in high school. But when Peyton left Cloverdale, she'd shed her old life, not keeping in touch with anyone except her mother. "I'm sorry," Peyton began.

"It's okay. I get it," Courtney said quickly. "You became a big star and forgot about all of us little people."

"It's not like that," Peyton said, tucking a strand of hair behind her ear. Geez! Coming home was getting stickier by the day.

Courtney laughed. "I'm just teasing. No hard feelings." She winked at Trevor. "I love watching her squirm." A coy smile tipped Courtney's lips. "So this is the famous Trevor Spencer."

Trevor smiled. "In the flesh."

"I love your Southern accent. It's got a sexy ring to it."

"Okay," Trevor said, amusement crossing his features.

Peyton chuckled to herself. Everywhere they went, the ladies flocked to Trevor, and Courtney was no exception. "I was just about to get us some Perrier. Would you like one?"

Courtney nodded, then boomeranged her attention right back to Trevor. Peyton was starting to feel like the third wheel.

After they drank the Perrier, Trevor excused himself to take a shower, probably because Courtney was so laser-focused on him it was sucking him dry.

"He's a hottie," Courtney said, watching him stride into the house. She leaned back in the chair, stretching her legs. "So, what's the scoop? Are you two an item?"

Peyton thrust out her lower lip, feeling a bit like she was still in high school. "None of your business."

Courtney grinned, shaking her head. "You haven't changed a bit. As evasive as always."

"Hey, that's not fair. We haven't seen each other for years, and you're asking me something personal."

"And whose fault is that?"

"That you're asking me something personal? Yours."

Courtney's face fell. "No, that we haven't seen each other in years."

Peyton bit back a smile. It was fun to razz Courtney, and she loved how they'd slipped effortlessly back into their old banter. Sitting on the front porch with Courtney, Peyton could almost imagine they were still teenagers and her mother would walk through the front door any minute, announcing dinner was ready. A pang shot through her.

Courtney shot her a concerned look. "You okay?"

"Yeah." Peyton hesitated, trying to gain control of her emotions. "It's hard not having my mom here."

Compassion colored Courtney's eyes as she nodded. "I'm sorry I couldn't be here for the funeral. I was out of town on a business trip."

Peyton shrugged. "I completely understand." It was then Peyton realized she'd not asked Courtney anything about herself. Judging by the way she was fawning over Trevor, Peyton assumed she wasn't married or in a relationship. "What do you do for a living?"

"I handle the marketing for several wineries."

"That's neat."

Courtney smirked. "Well, it's not as great as having your own TV show, but I guess it's okay."

The small jabs were wearing on Peyton's nerves. She looked Courtney in the eye. "Look, I know you're ticked because I left town without saying anything, and didn't keep in touch. But I was dealing with a lot of stuff."

"Carter."

"Yeah," she finally said after a long pause.

"What happened between the two of you? One minute you were getting married, and the next you disappeared."

"Things just didn't work out." She forced a smile. "Let's just leave it at that. I really am very sorry I hurt you. It wasn't intentional. You were a good friend to me."

Courtney's features softened ever so slightly. "Hey," she said brightly, touching Peyton's arm. "Are you going to the Websters' party next weekend?"

Peyton's eyes widened. "No."

"Well, you should." She gave Peyton a sly look. "Unless you're still hung up on Carter Webster."

Heat rose in Peyton's cheeks. "No. Absolutely not," she huffed.

Courtney laughed. "Ah, methinks thou doth protest too much."

"Now you're starting to sound like Mr. Labrum."

"Oh, speaking of Mr. Labrum, did you know he's legally blind?"

The breath left Peyton's lungs. "Are you serious?"

"Yeah. Macular degeneration I believe."

"That's so sad. He's a good man."

"He's okay, I guess. If you're into poetry and all that mumbo jumbo."

It irked Peyton that Courtney was so blasé about Mr. Labrum's plight. But then again, she'd been in Cloverdale the entire time, whereas for Peyton, everything was fresh.

"Well, if you don't go to the Websters' party, you should at least attend the annual service auction held at the high school."

"When is it?"

"This Thursday."

Peyton thought for a minute. "I don't remember Cloverdale doing any type of service auction."

"It started three years ago when Principal Jacobs had a heart attack."

"He did?"

Courtney chuckled. "Yeah, he did. Did you think life for everyone in Cloverdale would just stop when you left town?"

"No, not at all. I just simply didn't realize he'd had a heart attack." She eyed Courtney. "Why are you acting so defensive about everything?"

"I'm not."

They sat there, each of them refusing to back down. Finally, Courtney spoke. "Anyway, Principal Jacobs was on his roof, laying shingles, when he had the heart attack. So a few of us put together an auction to help raise money to help with his medical bills, replace his roof, and do a few other repairs on his home. It was so successful, we decided to continue the tradition. Each year we pick a few families in need to help."

"That's fantastic."

"I'm in charge this year, and I could use your support. Will you come?"

"Hmm ... I'll think about it."

Courtney rolled her eyes. "I know that look."

Coming home had been hard enough. Peyton didn't know if she was ready to go back to her old high school and mingle with townsfolk. But if she was going to create a thriving bed and breakfast, attending the service auction was a great way to start. Her plan was to get the bed and breakfast up and running, then hire a capable manager to take over while she continued doing her show in Texas. She realized Courtney was watching her, waiting for an answer. "Okay, I'll go."

A broad smile split Courtney's lips. "Awesome. Will you come to the Websters' party too?"

Peyton scowled. "Don't push it."

CHAPTER 5

*P*ulling into the high school parking lot, Peyton checked her makeup in the rearview mirror. She'd hoped Trevor would accompany her tonight, but he stayed home to rest. Not that she blamed him. They'd been working like crazy.

Peyton wished she could've stayed home too. Too bad she promised Courtney she'd come.

The high school and gym looked exactly as she remembered. It seemed like only yesterday that she and other seniors had a water balloon fight in the parking lot.

She had to laugh when her palms went sweaty. As much as she was in the public eye, she would've thought she had nerves of steel. But she was antsy about going to a silly service auction in a small town. Who was she kidding? Here, in this valley, it was impossible to separate the girl she once was from the woman she'd become. These people knew her as the poor girl who'd somehow managed to snag the most eligible bachelor in town. The girl who lived in constant fear of what havoc her alcoholic stepfather might wreak. Some of the people in this town had not been very kind to her when she was growing up. What would she find tonight? Acceptance or more rejection?

JENNIFER YOUNGBLOOD & SANDRA POOLE

She straightened her shoulders, resolved to see it through … for better or worse. She said under her breath. "I am who I am, like it or not."

As luck would have it, Carter was one of the first people she saw when she stepped through the doors. It had not even entered her mind that he would be here tonight. The Carter she remembered wasn't overly concerned about civic matters. Then again, this was a little different because it involved direct service to individuals. And as much as it pained her to admit it, Carter had always been generous.

Their eyes met, sending a jolt through her. He was as handsome as ever, wearing a white button-up shirt, jeans, and a gray sports jacket, the exact color of his eyes. As usual, his dark blond hair had just the right amount of wave to make it look fashionably messy. He acknowledged her presence with a slight nod before turning away.

His reaction felt like a snub, irritating the heck out of her. She had a good mind to march over to him this instant and demand that he tell her what he was planning to do about the house. Surely he'd seen the construction taking place. He had to know she was moving ahead with the renovation.

She shook her head, focusing instead on finding a seat amidst the rows of chairs facing the stage on the back wall. She spotted Courtney on the stage, looking chipper in a red pantsuit.

She scanned the crowd, recognizing only a handful of faces— mostly former teachers and coaches. There was a time when she knew almost everyone in town. The dynamics must've changed more than she realized in the past five years. She felt intensely out of place as she navigated through the crowd, making a beeline for a seat on the back row.

"Peyton!" Carter's voice penetrated the noise. Peyton stopped, looking his direction.

He flashed a friendly smile, like they were nothing more to each other than old buddies. "Come over here. I want to introduce you to someone."

She stood for a minute, wondering what he was up to, before making her way over to him.

A tall, fashionably dressed blonde stood beside him.

"Peyton, this is Millicent. Millicent ... Peyton."

A cheerful smile stretched over Millicent's face as she extended a slender hand. "It's nice to meet you, Peyton." Then her eyes widened in recognition. "Oh my gosh! You're Peyton Kelley from *Fix It Up*. I just love your show." She turned to Carter. "Shame on you. You didn't tell me you were friends with a TV star."

"It must've escaped my mind," Carter said dryly, looking at Peyton.

Millicent reached in her purse. "Do you mind if I take a picture with you?"

Peyton was amused. "Not at all."

Millicent thrust her phone at Carter. "Here ... you take it."

He snapped the picture and handed the phone back to Millicent.

"So, Carter tells me you two are old high school chums," Millicent said, linking a protective arm through Carter's.

The pang of jealousy that stabbed through Peyton caught her off guard. She looked at Carter, sensing his unease. "Yeah, you could say that. I'm Carter's ex-fiancée," she said, using the matter-of-fact tone Carter had used when he said those same words to Trevor.

Millicent's face fell, and she turned to Carter for an explanation. But he just stood there, studying Peyton, an unreadable expression on his face.

Peyton looked him in the eye. "We need to talk soon about the house ... sooner rather than later."

He nodded, his jaw taut.

Millicent's expression had changed from one of admiration to suspicion, but Peyton smiled through the tension. "Well, it was nice meeting you, Millicent. If you'll excuse me, I need to find a seat." She gave Carter a final nod before turning on her heel and sauntering away.

Peyton sat down in a chair. Out of the corner of her eye, she saw Carter and Millicent sit down at the end of her row. What was the deal with the two of them? They were obviously a couple. Were they dating or engaged? Millicent seemed to be cut from the same high-society cloth as Carter. Kathryn Webster would no doubt be pleased about the union. A bitter taste rose in Peyton's mouth as the old hurts came rushing back. Thankfully, before she could dwell too much on past woes, Courtney stepped up to the microphone.

"Ladies and gentlemen, if I could please have your attention. The auction is about to begin, so take a seat and shush." she ordered, doing the universal movement to mime zipping her lips.

This brought a few chuckles from the crowd.

"We've had so many wonderful donations, and as you know, the proceeds will help various families. So open up your wallets and be generous with your time and skills. Lyle Summers has graciously agreed to be our auctioneer. Put your hands together for Lyle."

Applause rippled through the crowd as a tall, thin man with a mustache and goatee took his place at the microphone.

Peyton couldn't help but be impressed with the generosity of the town as Lyle auctioned off the items, which included baked goods, oil paintings, quilts, and birdhouses carved from wood. After the tangible items were auctioned off, Lyle asked for volunteers to donate their time and skills for specific services like pressure washing, painting, and light carpentry work. As the auction was nearing its close, Courtney reemerged on stage.

"Lyle, we really appreciate your help. Let's give him a round of applause."

Courtney waited until after the clapping died down before continuing. "We saved the best for last. Mr. Labrum, a former teacher at Cloverdale High, has a master bathroom that's in need of major repairs. Many of us in this gym had Mr. Labrum as a teacher."

A few whistles and yells went through the gym.

Peyton sat up in her seat.

"The master bathroom needs to be brought into compliance with handicap regulations." Courtney scanned the audience. "I'm thrilled to announce that one of our former classmates has graciously agreed to foot the cost of the entire remodel."

Murmurs rustled through the crowd.

A smile broke over Courtney's lips. "Carter Webster, come on up here."

Loud applause rippled through the audience as Carter walked to the stage.

Carter stepped up to the microphone. "Thank you."

More applause.

"Mr. Labrum's a good man and friend. He certainly taught me a lot, and he's an important part of our community. I'm grateful I can play a small part in helping repay him for his kindness."

The applause around Peyton was deafening as people stood. Conflicting emotions churned inside her. So there was still goodness in Carter, after all.

Carter grinned. "But wait, there's more," he teased. "We're fortunate to have a celebrity in our midst. An expert at remodeling homes."

Peyton tensed as blood pumped hard through her veins. Surely he wasn't talking about her.

Carter looked straight at her, pointing. "Peyton Kelly, come on up here."

All eyes turned to Peyton.

"Come on up," Carter urged. "Don't be shy."

Hesitantly, she stood. What was Carter up to?

Peyton's thoughts were in a jumble as she made her way to the stage, trying to be as dignified as she could under the circumstance.

She stepped up to Carter. "What's this about?" she whispered through clenched teeth.

He merely smiled and turned to the microphone. "Ladies and gentlemen, you all know our very own Peyton Kelly—star of *Fix It Up* on HGTV."

More applause.

Carter held up a hand to quiet the audience. "Peyton has agreed to spearhead the renovations on Mr. Labrum's master bathroom."

Shock rankled over Peyton, followed by anger.

"What're you doing?" she muttered, trying to figure out Carter's endgame. Was he trying to stall her own renovations to give him more time to convince her to sell him the house?

"Smile at the audience," Carter whispered. "You're doing something nice for the community. Look, there's Mr. Labrum on the front row."

Mr. Labrum's face radiated gratitude, his unseeing eyes covered with dark glasses as he clapped furiously. Her heart softened. Helping him was a good thing. But she didn't appreciate being tricked into it by the likes of Carter Webster.

Carter motioned to the microphone, a challenging look in his eyes. "Isn't there anything you'd like to add?"

She straightened her shoulders. Then she plastered on the face she often wore in front of the camera. "It's good to be back in Cloverdale. Mr. Labrum was always kind to me, and I'm grateful I can lend a helping hand." Then she had an idea. Something that would keep Carter close, allowing her to keep an eye on him so she wouldn't be worried what he was up to all the time. "Carter hasn't even told you the best part." She turned to him and winked. "It's okay. I'll tell them. Not only is Carter going to fund the project, but he's going to work as my assistant."

The crowd went wild.

Carter was surprised.

"That's my condition, hotshot," Peyton said, eyeing him.

A smile stole over his lips. "Your assistant, huh?"

She thrust out her chin. "Yep."

He sighed. "Okay, I'll do it. Just remember … it was your idea."

It occurred to Peyton that Carter didn't look upset about the situation. In fact, he looked rather pleased, giving her the sick feeling she'd somehow played right into his hands. What had she gotten herself into?

CHAPTER 6

*C*arter watched his mother pace back and forth in front of him.

"Have you lost your mind?" Kathryn's voice rose to a fevered pitch. "First you stop by Peyton's place, and now you're working with her on a renovation project for some blind man?"

"Not just some blind man," Carter countered, fighting to keep his voice even. "It's Art Labrum, my former English teacher. He's a good man."

"I'm sure he's a peach," Kathryn fired back, "but that doesn't change the fact that you're putting yourself at risk by spending time with Peyton Kelly."

"Mother, you're overreacting."

She belted out a harsh laugh. "Am I? I got a call from Millicent just before you arrived. She was in tears. I had to assure her you no longer have feelings for Peyton and that the arrangement was purely for the good of the community." She glared at Carter. "Please tell me that's the truth."

"Yes, of course. It helps the community and us."

"Us? And just how do you figure that?"

"Working with Peyton will give me the opportunity to persuade her to sell. Right now, she'll hardly speak to me. But if we're together for several days on end, she'll be forced to deal with me."

Kathryn folded her arms over her chest, her long fingernails drumming on her arms as she gave him a probing look. "Are you sure this isn't some ploy to get Peyton back?"

Carter laughed. "Heck no! That was over eons ago."

Kathryn's eyes held his. "Are you sure?"

"Yes. I promise." He leaned in and kissed her on the cheek. "Don't worry, Mother. I've got the whole thing under control," he said, as he hurried out the door.

"Make sure you call Millicent and smooth things over," she called after him.

"Sure thing," he chimed.

Most of what he told his mother was true. He was going to try his best to convince Peyton to sell her half of the bed and breakfast. Long before the auction took place, he'd promised Courtney he would donate the funds to help Art Labrum. But the idea to have Peyton do the renovation only came to him when he saw the look on her face as Millicent slipped her arm through his. Peyton was jealous. And that could only mean one thing—she still had feelings for him.

TREVOR WAS NOT a happy camper when he found out about Mr. Labrum's remodel. Peyton could see his point, even though there was nothing she could do to change the situation. Trevor had dropped everything to help her with the bed and breakfast, and she was pulling off that to work on another project … with her ex-fiancé. The whole thing sounded absurd to Peyton, too. But it would give her a chance to convince Carter to sell his half.

Then, Trevor got a call from a client in Texas, asking him to remodel a family room. The timing was good, because Peyton estimated it would take Trevor about three weeks to complete the project. By that time, she hoped to be finished with Mr. Labrum's master bath so she could focus on the bed and breakfast.

Right before Peyton dropped Trevor off at the airport, he asked her a question that rattled her. "Look, I know the lines of our relationship often get blurred to the point where I'm not sure if we're just friends or something more. But tell me this ... do I need to be worried?"

Her brows furrowed. "About what?"

"You and Carter Webster."

Heat radiated through her as she scowled. "Heavens no! I can't stand the guy."

Trevor looked sad. "Just promise you'll tell me if something develops between the two of you."

She made a face. "Are you not listening to anything I'm saying? Nothing's gonna happen between me and Carter. The only reason I agreed to renovate Mr. Labrum's master bath was so I can convince the moron to sell his half of the bed and breakfast." She glowered. "So I can get him out of my life for good."

Trevor let out a breath. "Okay." He gave her a long look. "Take care of yourself."

Peyton got the crazy impression he was saying goodbye for good. A stone pit settled in her stomach. "You're coming back in three weeks, right?" She let out a shaky laugh. "We have a bed and breakfast to remodel and then season two of our show to think about."

"Of course." He smiled, touching her face.

She leaned over and gave him a tight hug. "Be safe, and text me when you get there so I'll know you arrived safely."

He was the first to pull away. "Will do." With that, he opened the car door and grabbed his luggage.

As Peyton watched him walk away, she was filled with an inexplicable sadness. Trevor was such a good guy—the kind of guy that didn't come along every day. She was lucky to have him in her life. He'd been super patient with her, but he wouldn't wait around forever. He was pulling away from her ... and of all things because of Carter; even though that was ancient history. Maybe, when Trevor came back from Texas, she should suggest they take their relationship to the next level. Yes, that was the answer. She couldn't allow her demons to keep her from losing her best friend. Relief settled over her as she put the car into drive and headed back to Cloverdale.

~

WHEN PEYTON PULLED into Mr. Labrum's driveway, Carter's Lamborghini was already there. It seemed so out of place in front of the modest home that it was almost laughable. Peyton doubted Carter had done a day's worth of manual labor his entire life. This was going to be interesting.

She rang the doorbell. Carter opened the door and ushered her in. She looked around, assessing the surroundings. The house was dated with dingy white tile and dark walls. It had a damp, musty smell, making Peyton wonder if there was a leak in the ceiling. Then she got a good look at Carter, who was wearing jeans and a white cardigan pullover. Peyton wrinkled her nose, shaking her head.

"What?"

"You're wearing that to work?" She chuckled. "It's obvious you haven't spent much time around construction."

He looked down at his sweater. "I assumed we'd spend most of today planning and shopping for supplies."

He did have a point, but she wasn't about to admit it.

Carter looked past her. "Where's your cowboy? I assumed he would come with you. The two of you seem inseparable on your show."

She tensed. "Are you referring to Trevor?"

"Well, yeah ... who else?"

"First of all, this arrangement has nothing to do with Trevor. Just because you roped me into it, doesn't mean Trevor has to suffer."

Carter's eyes narrowed. "I would hardly describe taking a little time out of your schedule to help an old friend remodel his bathroom as suffering."

Peyton met his accusation head-on as she leaned into his personal space, lowering her voice. "This charade has nothing to do with helping Mr. Labrum, and you know it. You arranged this entire thing to further your agenda."

His eyes hardened. "Oh yeah, and exactly what agenda would that be?"

Her jaw went slack. "Huh?"

"What agenda could I possibly have?" he pressed.

She tried to think. "Well, for starters, being here takes me away from working on my house."

"*Our* house."

She gritted her teeth. "You know what I mean." She'd forgotten how taxing it was to go head-to-head with Carter. He was an expert at debate, turning things around to make her feel like she was in the wrong. No matter how plausible his arguments were, she had to keep reminding herself she was right.

"You never did answer my question."

This was getting ridiculous! "What question?"

"Where's Trevor?"

"It's none of your dang business. What's the matter, Carter? Afraid you'll get your hands dirty?" she taunted.

He laughed. "Just because you do remodeling on your little show doesn't mean you hold the monopoly on work."

"We'll see," she countered icily.

"Let's just do what we came here to do, shall we?"

She motioned. "After you."

They stepped into the living room, where Mr. Labrum was sitting in a recliner. He was wearing the same thick glasses Peyton remembered, but his hair was considerably thinner. And he looked frail.

He turned his head in their direction, but Peyton could tell from the way he gazed past them that he couldn't see. "Hello, thanks for coming," he said, holding out his hand.

Peyton stepped up and grasped it in hers. "Mr. Labrum, it's so good to see you."

"It is great to see you too," he responded automatically, then chuckled. "Poor choice of words. I should clarify that statement. 'We were put into our bodies, as fire is put into a pan to be carried about;

53

but there is no accurate adjustment between the spirit and the organ.' Ralph Waldo Emerson."

A smiled tugged at Peyton's lips. "Still quoting poetry, I see."

"It's in the blood, I am afraid. My eyes may have failed me, but my mind is still intact … thank the Lord. Have a seat." He removed the book from his lap and placed it on the nearby side table. "Braille," he explained. "I'm still trying to learn it, but it's not as easy as it looks." He laughed at his own joke.

Peyton sat down on the sofa and assumed Carter would sit in the chair on the opposite side of the room. She was surprised when he sat down on the other end of the sofa. Being here with him in this intimate setting was surreal and unnerving. It didn't help that she was acutely aware of his every move. And to make matters worse, he was even more devastatingly handsome now than he was when they were engaged. In that regard, time had been very good to Carter Webster.

"You're probably wondering why I still wear my glasses," Mr. Labrum said.

She should've wondered that, but she was so flustered by Carter that she didn't even think about it.

"My glasses are a part of me. I feel naked without them. And I can still see things in my peripheral vision. It's my direct vision that has been affected by the deterioration of the central portion of the retina. For instance, I can see the outline of your shoulders and arms, but there's a blur over your face, like someone took an eraser and smudged it out."

Compassion welled in Peyton's breast. "I'm so sorry."

He waved away the comment. "I'm not the only one affected by the disease. Macular degeneration is one of the leading causes of vision loss, affecting millions of Americans. That's more than cataracts and glaucoma combined."

Peyton's eyes went wide. She felt like she was listening to an infomercial. Then she caught Carter's eye and realized he was thinking the same thing. He winked, sending a burst of warmth over her. The connection between them was so strong that it was almost like she'd never left Cloverdale and had been here with him all along.

The distance between them seemed to shrink as her pulse increased. She broke the connection and looked away.

"Don't mind me," Mr. Labrum said, almost as if reading Peyton's mind. "I don't get many visitors, so when I do, I start carrying on about insignificant details. It drives my sister crazy." He paused. "Peyton, how have you been? I listen to your show regularly."

"Things are going okay."

"I was sorry to hear about the passing of your mom and stepfather."

"Thanks." She swallowed. It was still hard to talk about it.

"Rosemary was a bright pupil. She was one of my first students when I started teaching." He chuckled, remembering. "Of course, I wasn't much older than Rosemary at the time, but I thought I knew everything back then."

Peyton vaguely remembered her mother telling her she'd had Mr. Labrum as a teacher, but she'd forgotten about it until now. "That's neat that you taught my mom, too."

He rubbed a hand across his brow. "Let's see, the last time I saw you was at your pre-wedding party, I believe."

Peyton flinched. She didn't dare look at Carter but could imagine he was having the same reaction.

"You looked radiant that evening."

"Thank you," Peyton said.

"Tell me, Carter … is she still just as beautiful?"

Heat stung Peyton's face. Had Mr. Labrum really asked Carter that?

She expected Carter to come back with a smart-aleck answer and was shocked when he said, "Even more so now than she was then."

She turned to Carter, expecting a cut to follow, but the expression on his face was genuine.

Mr. Labrum nodded, a look of satisfaction on his face. "I thought that would be the case. You've come into your own."

"Thank you," Peyton said, not feeling that way at all. On the contrary, ever since she'd come back to Cloverdale, she felt lost—a fish out of water. And Carter thought she was even more beautiful now? She was strangely flattered and confused. The situation with Carter was so muddled she couldn't even begin to sort through her feelings. She jerked when she realized Carter was studying her. Then he smiled. Warmth flooded over her, followed by the disgusting burst of attraction she always felt in his presence. Had Peyton not heard and witnessed the things she had at their pre-wedding party, she could almost believe nothing had changed between them.

Mr. Labrum's pragmatic tone was the much-needed jolt that jerked Peyton back to reality. "Let me start by saying how much I appreciate what the two of you are doing. I know it's a sacrifice, especially for you, Peyton, to stop working on your own home and come here to help me."

Her eyes widened. Mr. Labrum had obviously overheard her and Carter arguing in the foyer.

"I'm glad I can help," she said quickly. "Really," she added with conviction.

"Me too," Carter added. He looked at Peyton and grimaced.

Peyton couldn't help but smile. Carter's expression was reminiscent of the conspiratorial way he used to look at her during the marathon lectures Mr. Labrum often delivered after catching them kissing in the supply cabinet. She shrugged off the thought. *So much for keeping her mind relegated to the present.*

Mr. Labrum clasped his hands. "Maybe you should look at the room and tell me what the options are."

"What would you like to have done?" Peyton asked, pulling a notebook from her workbag. She had learned it was beneficial to ask this question before asserting her own opinions.

"The tub is hard to get in and out of. I'm afraid I'll fall because I can't see. I'd like to replace it with a large shower. Then, I can get one of those handicap chairs and a sprayer."

"Do you have any ideas about the design scheme? How you would like it to look?" As soon as the words left her mouth, Peyton realized her folly. Her face flamed as she tried to undo the damage. "I-I mean, are there certain materials you would like to use?" she stammered, glancing at Carter, whose eyes were dancing with amusement.

Mr. Labrum didn't skip a beat. "No, I'll leave that to you. Carter's been here many times. He can show you the bathroom."

Peyton was surprised. "You come here often?" she asked Carter. "I didn't realize you and Mr. Labrum were such good friends."

Amusement crossed Carter's features. "Well, how could you know? You haven't been here."

The words stung like darts as Peyton shot him a scornful look.

"Now, Carter, don't be hard on Peyton. She's had a rough time dealing with the loss of her family members. And Peyton, please call me Art." He laughed. "I think we've outgrown the teacher/student relationship."

"Okay," Peyton said, feeling intensely awkward about the whole situation.

Carter motioned with his head. "This way."

After making a thorough assessment of the master bath, Peyton and Carter sat at the kitchen table, developing a plan of action while Mr. Labrum took a nap. Even though Mr. Labrum … Art … would only be able to catch glimpses of the finished project out of his peripheral vision, Peyton was determined to give him the best possible result. "What's the budget?"

Carter leaned back in his chair, waving a dismissive hand. "Whatever it takes."

She looked up from her notes. "I'm sorry?"

"I'll pay whatever it costs."

"Really?" She was impressed despite herself. "That's very generous."

"Art's a good friend, and he's been through a hard time. It's the least I can do." He quirked a smile. "After all, he did put up with the two of us in high school."

The wistful look in Carter's eyes brought a rush of emotion Peyton could scarcely contain. Being here with Carter made her feel more alive than she'd felt in years, and yet it was so painful. How easy it would be to reach across the table and brush aside the strand of dark blond hair that kept falling over his eye. She forced herself to look

57

away from his broad chest and the way the muscles moved under his shirt as he shifted. Geez! She was pathetic.

Get a grip! She clasped her hands tightly in her lap.

"So, what's the plan?"

Blood throbbed in her temples. That was an excellent question. What was her plan? Would she ever be able to eradicate Carter Webster from her thoughts and heart? Or was she doomed to carry around that baggage the rest of her life? Then she realized he was watching her, a trace of amusement coloring his eyes. She licked her dry lips. "Um ... the plan?"

"For the bathroom," he prompted.

She adopted her best professional tone to recover. "I know Art won't be able to see it, but I'd like to use whites and grays ... with a variety of textures. If we use the latest laminate flooring, it'll give the appearance of bamboo but will feel comfortable on his feet. We'll replace the bathtub with a large tiled shower." As she continued outlining the plans, Carter scooted his chair closer. She caught the faint whiff of his cologne mixed with his own scent, causing her breath to catch. When she hesitated, Carter gave her a funny look.

"Everything okay?"

She nodded. "Yeah ... just a little tired, I guess. That and the lack of a decent meal." When he looked puzzled, she added, "It's hard to eat properly when you have no kitchen."

"I see." He paused. "You're really good at design." He gave her an appraising look. "For what it's worth ... you've done well. Built a good life for yourself."

The compliment broadsided her. "Thanks."

He placed a hand over hers. "I mean it."

The longing in his eyes ignited a fire that made her heart pound so fiercely, she felt it was trying to claw out of her chest. The air held its breath as she looked at his lips, remembering how they felt against hers. Then, an unbidden image came to her mind, and she saw herself tearful and broken on the night of their engagement party. She'd trusted him so completely, and he betrayed her. She removed her hand from his, suddenly angry with herself and with Carter.

58

"Let's not forget what this is," she barked, her eyes filling with accusation.

A look of surprise flittered over his features as he shot her a hard look. "So are we gonna keep tiptoeing around what went wrong between us, or are we gonna get it out in the open?"

"No!" she blurted, fire in her eyes. "The past is over and done." Her hands started to shake, and she grasped her notebook to stop the motion, hoping Carter hadn't noticed. She took a calming breath. "Let's keep this professional. What're we going to do about the bed and breakfast?"

Time seemed to stand still as he looked at her. Then he chuckled. "Bed and breakfast? You mean the broken-down house?"

The disdain in his voice was oddly comforting, because it set her back on familiar ground. It was easier to loathe Carter than to remember how much she'd loved him. "I'm going to turn it into a bed and breakfast," she snapped. "That's what it was designed to be. The bones are already there."

"I'll pay you triple the value of the house. Think about how much money that is, Peyton. You can wash your hands of this town and never look back."

A furrow appeared between her brows. "Who says I want to do that?"

There was a subtle challenge in his eyes. "Don't you?"

"Yeah, sometimes," she admitted. She straightened her shoulders. "But like it or not, this place is my home. And that broken-down house, as you call it, is the only tangible thing I have left of my mother. I won't let you or anyone else destroy it." She stood, weary of the whole situation. "I think we've covered enough ground for one day."

"Typical."

The comment was like a red flag in front of a bull. "And what exactly do you mean by that?" she demanded.

He also stood. "When things get hard, you run away."

Fury splintered over her. "I'm not running away. I'm just stopping for today."

A hard smile spread over his lips. "Oh, no. We're not done. We still have to shop for materials and make arrangements to have the bathroom demolished down to the studs." He leaned into her personal space. "Not afraid of a little work ... are you Peyton?"

She wanted to slap the smug expression off his face. "Not on your life," she slung back.

"Then what're we waiting for? Let's get it taken care of."

"Fine," she huffed.

"We'll take my car."

"Like we're going to pick up construction materials in a Lamborghini. Right!"

"Ever heard of delivery? Geez, Peyton, you'd never know you did this for a living. Do I have to do everything for you?"

THEY DROVE in stony silence until Carter pulled up in front of a familiar pasta and pizza shop. Peyton's heart nearly stopped. "What're you doing?"

Carter turned off the engine. "Getting something to eat."

"What kind of game are you playing?"

Carter was all innocence. "No game. I'm hungry, and it's lunchtime."

"We never agreed on lunch."

He rolled his eyes. "Lunch isn't something you have to agree on. It takes place around the same time every day."

"Stop it," she snapped. "Of all the places to take me. Here? Where we had our first date?" Oops, she shouldn't have said that. Now he was going to think she cared enough to remember.

"Oh ... we did? I'd forgotten about that."

"Sure you did." She folded her arms tightly over her chest.

Carter let out a long sigh. "Look, the hostility has got to stop. If we're going to work together, we need to find some common ground."

"Like that's gonna happen," she retorted.

He opened his car door. "I'm going inside to get something to eat.

The reasonable thing to do would be to come with me. But if you'd rather wait here, that's your prerogative."

Her jaw dropped. "Are you serious? You're the one who insisted we get materials. Then you announced you were driving."

"Are you hungry or not?"

"Yeah, I'm hungry."

"Okay, let's get something to eat. No hidden agenda. Promise. Just pizza and pasta."

Her eyes narrowed as she studied him.

"Suit yourself," he said as he got out.

She threw her door open, jumped out, and slammed it shut. "You're not leaving me in the car!"

He motioned. "After you."

CHAPTER 7

*P*eyton ignored the curious glances she and Carter received as the hostess led them to a table. News traveled so quickly through the Cloverdale grapevine, Peyton imagined the whole town would be talking about seeing them together by nightfall. When they were seated, the pretty brunette flashed Carter a warm smile. "It's so good to see you today, Carter. It's been a while since you've been in. I've missed you," she said, a hint of longing in her voice.

"Good to see you too, Lynn," he said casually. "Things have been a little hectic lately."

She touched his arm. "Well, don't be a stranger. You're welcome here anytime." Her eyes carried an innuendo that seemed lost on Carter. "Our special today is calzones. Your server will be right with you." She nodded coolly at Peyton before sashaying away.

Peyton arched an eyebrow. "She seems quite taken with you. Maybe we should ask her to pull up a chair and join us."

A lopsided smile touched his lips. "Not jealous, are you?"

"Not hardly," Peyton quipped, feeling like she'd slipped back in time. How many times had they had this same conversation? Too many times to count. And to make matters worse, the table where they'd sat on their first date was directly across from them.

Carter followed her vision and instantly picked up on her train of thought. "It feels like it was another lifetime, doesn't it?"

"Yes," she said quietly, "and yet, it looks exactly the same."

He chuckled. "I don't think Brian has done any updates in decades, so it probably is the same."

A feeling of melancholy settled over Peyton. She and Carter had shared such dreams and aspirations ... and it all went up in smoke. This little trip down memory lane was starting to take its toll, leaving her feeling zapped. She didn't know how much more of the emotional roller coaster she could take.

Carter reached for her hand. When she tried to pull away, he held it tight. "Hey ..." he began, holding her eyes.

"Don't." She swallowed hard, commanding the tears to dry.

"Just hear me out, okay?" His eyes searched hers. "Please?"

Her jaw tightened as she nodded.

"I want you to forget everything that happened between us in the past."

She let out an incredulous laugh. He might as well have asked to her to forget her own name.

"I'm serious. Let's start fresh. We're simply two professionals working on a project together. We'll do Art's bathroom, then decide what to do about our house."

She'd not missed his reference to *our* house, suggesting an intimate connection. "Professionals, huh? Have you even worked on a house before?"

Frustration tinged his features. "I can hold my own. Now, what do you say? We'll both be nervous wrecks if we keep dredging up the past day in and day out."

Peyton mulled over his suggestion. Could it work? Maybe. If she started thinking of Carter as a mere coworker, it might help her navigate through this whole ordeal. At this point, they had nothing to lose. Then she looked down and realized he was still holding her hand. "So, do you always hold your coworkers' hands?"

He chuckled nervously. "Good point." He let go. Then he held out his hand. "Hello, I'm Carter Webster, a close friend of Art Labrum. It's a pleasure to work with you on his project."

She just sat there, looking at him.

"Don't leave me hanging," he urged.

She rolled her eyes. "This is ridiculous."

He wiggled his eyebrows, looking boyishly adorable. "Come on, Peyton, shake my hand. You know you want to."

"Fine," she grumbled, putting her hand in his.

He gave it a hearty shake, and then promptly let it go. "It's nice to meet you," he said cheerily. "The Pizza Shack has been a staple in Cloverdale for years. I highly recommend the supreme pizza with the Italian salad. But the pepperoni and honey is good too."

Despite her best efforts to quell it, a laugh bubbled in her throat, dispelling the gloom. "It's nice to meet you, Carter. I'm Peyton Kelly."

"Kelly," he mused, scratching his head. "You know, I have some neighbors by that name. Are you by any chance related to them?"

She laughed. "Absolutely not."

"I didn't think so."

She relaxed in her seat, suddenly feeling hungry. "A supreme pizza sounds good. But we'd better make it a small. I've heard this place is legendary for their shakes, and I wanna save room for dessert."

PEYTON FOUGHT off a shiver as she reached for her fleece jacket draped over the back of her chair and slipped it on. The sun had fallen behind the hills half an hour ago, leaving a chill in the evening air. Peyton leaned back, drinking in the splashes of color from the leaves on the fat purple grape clusters. Her gaze followed the gentle slope of the land to the trees framing the vineyard, their leaves ablaze with splendid colors. Then she looked toward the rolling mountains beyond, cradled by the sky darkening to indigo. After being in Texas, where everything was dry and flat, she had a new appreciation for this picturesque land with its protective hills.

A flame flickered cheerily from the burning candle in the center of the outdoor patio table, lending a coziness to the evening. She looked at Courtney, who helped herself to a third taco. This was the second time the two of them had gotten together for dinner this week, and Peyton appreciated the company. With Trevor gone, the house was lonely, so when Courtney called and offered to bring tacos, Peyton readily agreed.

"When's Trevor getting back in town?"

"I'm not sure. It depends on when he finishes his project."

"You must miss him," Courtney said, a little too casually.

"Yeah, a little." Peyton shot Courtney a sly look. "So, are you asking for me or you?"

Courtney's deep blush answered Peyton's question. She didn't blame Courtney for crushing on Trevor. He was handsome, funny, witty, kind. Peyton stopped. He possessed all the qualities that mattered. In fact, had she not been so hurt by Carter, she probably would've already fallen head over heels for him herself. Peyton wasn't the least bit surprised when Courtney changed the subject.

"Doesn't it bother you to sleep in the bed and breakfast alone?"

"Yeah, it's a little uncomfortable, I suppose. But what other choice do I have?"

Courtney's eyes grew round as she leaned forward, lowering her voice. "Do you think Karen Sandburg really saw a ghost?"

Peyton's brows drew together. "What're you talking about?"

"Oh, I thought you knew."

"Knew what?"

"Before you got back into town, Karen and her husband, Scott, were doing some work on the house."

"I know, I hired them." It was hard enough for Peyton to return home to face her mother's death. She couldn't face packing up her and Harold's belongings, so she'd hired the Sandburgs to do it for her. Peyton knew she'd eventually have to go through everything piece by piece to sort the keepsakes from the junk, but that could wait until she was emotionally ready to tackle the project.

"Anyway," Courtney continued, "according to what I heard, Karen was working in the attic when she heard someone crying. She went downstairs to see if it was Scott, but he was perfectly fine. On her way back to the attic, she caught a glimpse of an old lady going around the corner."

A shiver ran down Peyton's spine. "The Sandburgs didn't mention that to me."

"Well, it was a big deal. Karen left the house that minute and refused to go back. Poor Scott had to finish the job alone."

Peyton scrunched her nose. "Are you sure someone's not pulling your leg?"

Courtney held up her right hand. "I swear, that's what I heard."

Annoyance crept over Peyton. The last thing she needed was Karen Sandburg spreading rumors about the bed and breakfast when she was trying to get the house remodeled and the business off the ground. "It sounds ridiculous."

Courtney gave Peyton a tentative look. "Um … forgive me for saying this, but do …" She hesitated, looking uncomfortable.

"Spit it out," Peyton prompted.

Courtney cleared her throat. "Do you think it could be your mother?"

Peyton's eyes went wide. Then she started laughing so hard tears came to her eyes. "That's the most ridiculous thing I've ever heard," she said, mopping her eyes.

Courtney's expression grew pinched. "Think about it—she died tragically before she had time to get her affairs in order. It's possible her spirit's in a state of unrest."

The wind picked up, sending a chill over Peyton. "Are you listening to yourself? I've never heard anything so absurd in my life!"

"There are inns all around the country that claim to be haunted. Who are we to say they're not?"

"Trust me. I've crawled over every inch of the place. If the bed and breakfast were haunted, I'd know it."

"All I'm saying is, I wouldn't want to spend the night there alone," Courtney said, suppressing a shudder.

"Well, lucky for you, you don't have to. And if you don't mind, I would appreciate it if you don't tell anyone else about the Sandburgs. I don't want rumors spreading. I've got enough to deal with without adding ghosts to my plate."

Courtney nodded in understanding. "Don't worry. I won't tell a soul. I just thought you ought to know." She paused. "Speaking of the other things you're dealing with—how's Carter?"

"Oh, you know Carter, same as always, I guess." Her feelings about Carter were mixed at the moment, but she didn't care to admit that to Courtney. The very morning after she told Carter she'd not had a decent meal since she ripped out her kitchen, she found a beautifully wrapped box containing a large blueberry muffin and a container of fresh fruit on her porch by the front door. When she asked Carter about it, he played dumb. But she was sure he was the one who'd left the food. For the past three days, a bakery item had been left on her front porch every morning. She was tempted to get up early to catch him in the act, but didn't want to jinx it. It was nice getting breakfast every morning, and it gave her something to look forward to— wondering what he'd leave next. Was this Carter's way of showing her he still cared? Maybe that was taking the sentiment a little too far. It was just breakfast, after all.

Courtney made a face. "I still can't believe Carter took you to The Pizza Shack where you had your first date."

"I was surprised too." She shrugged. "Then again, there aren't a lot of choices in Cloverdale. The Pizza Shack's one of, what, three places where you can go in and sit down. Other than the Websters' restaurants, of course. But those are all fine dining and only open for dinner."

"That's true." Courtney took a large bite of her taco. After she chewed and swallowed, she asked, "So how are things going with Mr. Labrum's bathroom?" She shook her head. "You could've blown me over with a feather when Carter volunteered you to do the work ... on stage, in front of the entire town."

Peyton scowled. "Yeah, he knew he had to do it that way. Otherwise, I would've flatly refused."

She gave Peyton a shrewd look. "Nah, you would've done it regardless."

Peyton's brows scrunched. "Why do you say that?"

"Because you have a soft spot for Mr. Labrum. And you like helping people."

"I do like to help people when I can. And I like Art. He's a good person, and he's been through a lot."

Courtney wrinkled her forehead. "Oh, so it's Art now. Wow."

She frowned. "Oh, quit making something out of nothing. He asked me to call him Art. Which I was happy to do. We're all adults now." Peyton reached for a chip and dipped it in salsa before plopping it in her mouth.

Today marked the fourth day of Art's project, and she and Carter were making surprisingly good progress. Carter hired a crew to tear out the bathroom, allowing them to start with a clean slate. And while Carter didn't possess Trevor's carpentry skills, he was a hard worker and handy. She and Carter had held to their agreement, limiting conversation to the present, only discussing surface topics.

Peyton had forgotten how much fun it was to be around him. He had a knack for putting people at ease and was always cracking jokes. But it was only a matter of time before they would have to delve into a conversation about the bed and breakfast; then all semblance of good-will would fly out the window. She sighed, glancing toward Carter's enormous mansion, looming like a silent phantom over her house and property.

Courtney seemed to read her mind. "Have you and Carter reached an agreement about the bed and breakfast?"

"No, we agreed not to discuss it until after we finish Art's project."

"That's probably wise. Otherwise, you'll rip each other's heads off."

Peyton chuckled darkly. "Yeah." She paused, worry seeping over her. "I don't know that the two of us will ever be able to reach an agreement."

Courtney reached for her cup and took a long drink of Dr. Pepper. "You could always get an arbitrator."

Peyton frowned. "I don't think so. It would be nearly impossible to find someone who's not influenced by the Websters."

"You could use my uncle. He's always dealing with these types of matters. People go to him because they want to keep their disputes private, and they want to avoid expensive court costs."

"Hmm … Does he know the Websters?"

"I don't think so; he lives in San Francisco." She shrugged. "Anyway, it's just a thought … for what it's worth. My uncle's semi-retired, so I'm not even sure he's taking new clients. I could ask, if you'd like."

It was an intriguing idea. Peyton felt sure that any reasonable person outside of the Websters' long arm of influence would see things her way. After all, the bed and breakfast had been in her family for three generations. Going to an arbitrator would bring a swift resolve to the conflict. "Would you mind getting me your uncle's contact info?"

"Sure." Courtney finished the last bite of her taco and groaned, holding her stomach. "I was super hungry and ate too much. But it was so good."

"It was excellent," Peyton agreed. Nothing beat authentic tacos, beans, rice, and chips from the local street vendors.

Courtney pulled a metal patio chair next to her and propped up her feet. "So, are you up for a chick flick tonight?"

"That sounds great." A smile tugged at Peyton's lips. "That is, if you're not afraid a ghost will get you."

"That's so mean," Courtney huffed, folding her arms over her chest. "I should've bought some donuts."

"For the ghost? I don't think she would appreciate them."

Courtney rolled her eyes. "No, smart butt! I should've brought donuts for me."

"I thought you said you were stuffed."

Courtney grinned. "I am, but there's always room for dessert."

Peyton laughed. "Amen." Resuming her relationship with Courtney had been one of the bright spots about coming home. Trevor was her only friend in Texas, and he was great. But Peyton missed the association of hanging out with another girl.

Trevor had a short tolerance for chick flicks, and she certainly couldn't discuss the nuances of her relationship with Carter with him. She'd only spoken to Trevor once since he left, and the conversation had been strained. Hopefully, she could remedy the tension between them when he returned.

"Hey, what're you wearing to the Webster party tomorrow night?"

Peyton frowned. "I haven't even thought about it." She'd been adamantly against going until Art pulled her aside three days ago and asked if she would take him to the party.

"I really want to go, but I need someone to push my wheelchair."

She was surprised. "Why are you going in a wheelchair? Are you having trouble walking?"

"No, but I find it easier to just go in the chair. That way, I have less risk of falling."

Peyton didn't have the heart to turn him down. But ever since she agreed to go, a cloud of dread had been hanging over her. Going back to the Webster Mansion was sure to unearth old memories. And she would have to see Kathryn Webster. She scowled. No amount of time could diminish her dislike for Carter's mother. The woman was not only small-minded and snobby, but also deceitful, pretending to be Peyton's friend while stabbing her in the back.

"Are you okay?"

Peyton forced a smile. "Yeah, just not looking forward to tomorrow night."

"Oh, it'll be fine." Courtney gave Peyton a reassuring smile. "Trust me ... you'll see."

CHAPTER 8

arter watched the server place their plates on the table. The restaurant was known for its steak and wine. Millicent took to the wine while he preferred the steak, which was why they ate here most nights.

Millicent took a drink from her wineglass, her lips forming a sultry pout as she looked icily across the table at Carter. "I can't believe you're working on a project with Peyton Kelly." The way she spat out Peyton's name made it sound dirty.

She pushed a lock of hair off her shoulder, her expression one of disdain. "Everyone's talking about it. And everyone saw you two together at The Pizza Shack. I'll bet your poor mother's freaking out."

"My mother's just fine," Carter countered, giving Millicent a steely look. "And I don't give a flying flip about what people are saying."

Her jaw dropped, worry clouding her pretty features. "But what about me? Do you care what I think?"

"Of course."

Relief eased the worry on her face as she smiled. "Good." She pushed the roasted potatoes around her plate with a fork. "How are things going with the renovation?"

Carter took a bite of his steak, appreciating the juicy flavor of the warm meat. "Very well. We should be able to wrap things up by the end of next week."

"That's fantastic," Millicent beamed, taking a generous bite of green beans. "Then you won't have to spend any more time with *her*." She sighed. "I still don't see why you got her to help with the renovation."

"Because Peyton's good at what she does, and I need her expertise to make sure the work is done correctly."

"There are plenty of designers who are just as capable as Peyton Kelly," she pouted.

Carter's grip tightened on his fork as he remained silent. He had no intention of explaining himself to Millicent. As he watched her pick at her roll with perfectly molded acrylic nails, taking microscopic bites because she was afraid of gaining an ounce, he couldn't help but remember how Peyton had eaten a normal-sized portion of lunch at The Pizza Shack. And then they'd had milkshakes for dessert.

Millicent was a beautiful woman with her crystal blue eyes, long lashes, and milky skin. Her figure was flawless, as was her hair and makeup. However, none of it was natural—she spent a fortune to have her hair done just right, and she had eyelash extensions and Botoxed lips. From the looks of her, Carter suspected she'd also had a boob job and possibly a few other things done to maintain that flawless Barbie doll appearance.

Peyton's beauty, on the other hand, was natural. When they were working, she kept her thick tresses pulled back in a simple ponytail. Her nails were blunt cut and polish free. Her vivid eyes were framed with naturally thick lashes. Her petite figure curved in all the right places, but she wasn't plastic-looking.

And he loved how Peyton went to the heart of the matter. If he'd been dating Peyton and the situation were reversed, Peyton wouldn't be sitting here pouting. She would've chewed him up one side and down the other for spending so much time with another woman.

"What's so funny?" Millicent wanted to know.

"Nothing."

"Are you excited about the party tomorrow?"

"Yes. Actually, I am." Mostly because Peyton was coming. He'd talked Art into persuading Peyton to take him. He knew Peyton well enough to know that the only way she would come was if she felt obligated to help Art. Okay, it was a sneaky thing to do, but he wanted Peyton to be there.

At first, he'd wanted Peyton to come so he could parade Millicent around, to prove he was over Peyton. But now, that no longer seemed important. Spending time with Peyton the past week had been exhilarating. He'd made a point of steering the conversation toward safe topics.

During their initial meeting at Art's house, when they were sitting at the kitchen table, Peyton nearly lost it when he asked her to tell him what went wrong between them. He was both intrigued and bothered by her reaction. Peyton was acting like she was the victim. But if Carter pressed her about it, she might clam up and refuse to see him. His only course of action was to bide his time; help her feel relaxed and comfortable around him. That's why he razzed her about the bed and breakfast, telling her how shabby it was. He knew the only way to put her at ease was to make her fighting mad. Peyton was a complex woman—an intriguing mix of tender and tough. He'd spoken the truth when Art inquired about Peyton's beauty. She was even more beautiful now than she'd been when they were young.

And he knew who *wouldn't* be at the party: Trevor. Was Trevor even still in town? He'd not seen hide nor hair of the man since they started working on Art's project. Peyton rarely spoke of him.

"Hey, you're in another world. Is everything okay?" Millicent asked.

"Everything's great."

"Good. I was thinking about wearing a yellow dress tomorrow. Do you think that's appropriate? I can pair it with my yellow wedges."

"Sounds great," he said, taking another bite of steak.

"Or I could wear my white silk shirt with the matching skirt. Should I wear my hair up or down? I was thinking I'd wear those dangly earrings you got me for my birthday."

Her mouth moved a mile a minute. Carter's mind went on autopi-

73

lot, returning to Peyton as he nodded and inserted the occasional word in the proper place. Millicent was so caught up in her monologue she didn't even notice.

A THOUSAND MEMORIES assaulted Peyton as she wheeled Art through the gate and along the path leading to the courtyard of the Webster Mansion. The soft music from the orchestra was reminiscent of the night of her pre-wedding party. For a minute, she found it hard to breathe.

"Are you okay?" Art asked when she halted in her tracks.

"Yes, I'm fine," she said tersely, shuffling forward.

He cleared his throat and began quoting:

"Fear no more the frown of the great,

Thou art past the tyrant's stroke; ...

Fear no more the lightning-flash,

Nor the all-dread thunder-stone;

Fear not slander, censure rash;

Thou hast finished joy and moan:

All lovers young, all lovers must

Consign to thee, and come to dust.

"SHAKESPEARE," he added.

Now was not the time for Art to wax philosophical. "Thank you, Art, that was a lovely recitation. But I'm afraid all the literature in the world's not gonna to help me tonight," she mumbled.

"Sorry, I'm afraid I get a little long-winded from time to time."

She instantly felt guilty for making him feel bad. "No, it's not you, but me," she said, tightening her jaw. She was surprised when he reached back and caught her hand.

"You can do this. You're stronger than you think."

She jerked, tears springing to her eyes. She was startled that he'd so accurately picked up on her feelings. "Thank you," she said quietly.

"Do you know anything about the history of this mansion?" he asked, as they started moving again.

"Not really," she responded, grateful he'd steered the conversation to a safe topic.

His voice took on the tone of a teacher as he continued, "The mansion was inspired by the Tuscan villa where Carter's maternal grandparents, Walter and Henrietta Spindleton, spent their honeymoon. They purchased the vineyards and winery in the '70s and tore down the existing structure, building the mansion in its place."

"Figures," Peyton muttered. It seemed Carter's family had a long-standing tradition of tearing down what they deemed to be useless to make way for their grandiose plans.

"I'm sorry, I didn't catch that," Art said.

"Nothing," she said quickly, looking up at the imposing structure beside them. When Peyton was young, the Webster Mansion had looked like something straight out of a fairy tale. She would sit on her tire swing for hours, staring up at it, wondering what it must be like to live here. It dawned on her that as close as she and Carter once were, Peyton had only been to the Webster Mansion a handful of times. Kathryn Webster had always been adamantly against her and Carter's relationship, so they'd steered clear of the place.

It was interesting to see the mansion through the seasoned eyes of a decorator. The mansion had a heavy neo-Gothic influence with its sweeping arches and vaulted ceilings. If Peyton had been designing it, she would've toned down the bright turquoise color of the shutters and painted the wrought iron a dark brown instead of the harsh black. Everything else, she would've left as it was.

They rounded the corner, and Peyton's breath caught as she looked at the pool and courtyard, which looked almost exactly as it had the night of the party on the eve of her and Carter's scheduled wedding. The same twinkling lights. The same thin, gauzy fabric. The same stage where Carter had publicly declared his love for her. Then Harold showed up and everything fell apart.

Tremors started in her hands, and she clutched the handles of the wheelchair to stay them. If she hadn't promised Art she would bring him to the party, she would've left that instant.

"Where would you like to go first?" she asked, focusing her attention on his needs rather than her demons.

"Would you mind wheeling me over to an empty table? Then you can fix me a plate and maybe get a glass of Cabernet Sauvignon," he said eagerly. "The Webster Wineries are known for their outstanding Cabernet Sauvignon and Chardonnay. You really should try it."

"Thanks, but I don't drink."

He chuckled. "Okay, then. I'll drink enough for the both of us. There are few pleasures left to a man in my condition … and you're the one driving."

She laughed. "Yes, I am. This is your night, Art. Enjoy it." She found an empty table and maneuvered him next to it.

Art began moving his hand to the beat of the music, as if he were conducting a symphony. He sighed appreciatively. "Debussy. One of my favorites. A child prodigy, sent to the Paris Conservatory at age eleven to study music."

Before Art could launch into an oration on the composer's life, Peyton touched his arm. "I'll be back in a few minutes with your food and wine."

"Thank you," he said, so appreciatively that it made Peyton feel guilty for wallowing in her sorrows. Art was almost completely blind, and yet he still managed to find enjoyment in life's simple pleasures.

Peyton took Art's plate to him and was standing in line at the bar to get him a glass of wine when she saw Carter standing near the stage. She sucked in a breath. He still had the power to make her go weak in the knees. Impeccably dressed in a white tux and black bowtie, his wavy hair was gelled for the occasion, emphasizing his prominent cheekbones and strong jaw.

Jealousy stabbed through Peyton when the stunning blonde by his side linked her arm through his and whispered something in his ear, causing him to laugh. Peyton recognized her as the same woman Carter was with at the auction: Millicent. Peyton was disappointed with herself for being jealous. Why did she care who Carter was with?

The two of them were through. The sooner she got that through her thick skull, the better off she'd be. At that moment, she missed Trevor and wished he was here. It was so awkward facing these people alone.

Her blood nearly stopped when Carter looked across the space and caught her watching him. He smiled, lighting his features.

She returned the smile with a tight one of her own and turned away, heat stinging her cheeks. How embarrassing! She was almost to the front of the line when she felt a tug on her arm and realized Carter was standing beside her.

"Hey, I'm surprised to see you here," he said.

"You knew I was bringing Art."

"No, I'm surprised to see you standing in line for wine. Surely you haven't taken up drinking since we've been apart." He clucked his tongue. "What's the world coming to?"

Her eyes rounded. "This isn't for me, it's for Art," she rushed to explain, then realized he was teasing her.

She laughed and shook her head.

"You look gorgeous. Red was always one of your best colors."

"Thank you," she murmured, feeling oddly pleased at the compliment.

Carter looked around. "Speaking of Art, where is he?"

Peyton pointed. "At a table. I took him a plate of food, but he wanted some wine. Evidently, you have a killer Cabernet Sauvignon he's dying to try."

Carter chuckled. "Yes, we do."

A few seconds later, it was Peyton's turn at the bar. Before she could give the bartender her request, Carter spoke. "We'll have a bottle of the Cabernet Sauvignon."

"Of course, Mr. Webster."

Peyton gave Carter a questioning look.

He winked. "Art's very fond of his wine. Giving him a bottle will save you the trouble of making a dozen repeat trips to the bar."

"Thank you."

When she reached for it, he shook his head. "I'll walk over there with you. I'd like to say hello to Art."

77

"Okay."

All eyes seemed to be glued to them as they walked over to the table, where Carter greeted Art.

"Thank you for the wine," Art said, his hand encircling the bottle, "my trusty company for the evening."

The corners of Peyton's lips turned down. "Hey, what about me? Am I not good company?"

Art laughed. "Yes, indeed. I meant no offense." His vacant eyes searched the space in front of him. "Carter?"

"I'm here."

"Peyton and I were just talking about dancing."

"We were?" Peyton said dubiously.

"Yes, Peyton was telling me how much she loves to dance."

"I remember," Carter said, his eyes meeting hers.

Peyton's pulse quickened. She was acutely aware of Carter's nearness and how the tiny lines around his eyes crinkled when he smiled. The perceptive look in his smoky gray eyes. The rough, tumbled look of his stubble and how he somehow managed to make it look elegant. The way his muscles moved underneath his tux.

"Yes," Art said. "I would dance every dance with the beautiful Peyton if I could. But alas, not only would I tumble over my own two feet, but endanger the other guests as well. Would you be a gent and dance with her ... on my behalf?"

"That's not necessary," Peyton countered, her cheeks growing warm. Then she saw amusement in Carter's eyes. "What?" she demanded.

Carter shrugged, a smile tugging at his lips, as he held out his hand. "For Art?" A challenge glittered in his eyes as he leaned closer. "Unless you're afraid."

She lifted her chin. "Not in the slightest," she quipped, placing her hand in his. When his fingers closed around hers, old, familiar feelings welled, and she got the impression nothing between them had changed. For a moment, she forgot about the people around them as he led her to the dance floor.

He placed an arm around her waist, pulling her close and sending a jolt of electricity buzzing through her veins; she gasped softly.

His eyes captured hers. "Dancing is like riding a bike," he murmured in her ear. "You never forget."

The promise in his voice sent delicious tingles circling down her spine as they danced in perfect sync. Peyton had the feeling she'd left reality and entered some shadowy world that was a mixture of her fiercest longings and deepest fears. Carter was her greatest weakness and no matter how hard she tried, she couldn't erase her need for him. The best she could do was figure out how to come to terms with it.

Carter's arms remained around her when the song ended.

"Um, the music stopped," she said, biting her lower lip.

"You know, Art will never allow us to have just one dance."

She nodded, feeling foolish for forgetting herself. Carter was only dancing with her because Art insisted. She forced a smile. "Of course."

They continued dancing through that song and the next, until Kathryn Webster stepped up to them and tapped Carter on the shoulder.

"Sorry to interrupt," she said crisply, "but Millicent has been looking all over for you."

Carter nodded and reluctantly released Peyton.

Peyton felt the loss of his touch instantly as she looked at Kathryn, who was still just as beautiful as Peyton remembered, but older and more fragile. No, that wasn't exactly true. Kathryn's body might've been fragile, but her eyes were just as ruthless and unyielding as they ever were—radiating her disapproval of Peyton. An intense dislike splattered over Peyton as she gave Kathryn a direct look.

Kathryn smiled, her eyes remaining cold. "Peyton Kelly, I'd heard you were back in town. It's nice of you to join us this evening."

"Thank you."

She cocked her head, looking thoughtful. "But I must say, I'm surprised you could find time to break away from your show. It looks like it keeps you busy."

"I find time to take care of the things that are important," Peyton said evenly.

"And your co-star, Trevor Spencer? Is he here with you tonight?"

Peyton saw Carter's jaw tense. An interesting reaction for someone who'd wanted out of their former relationship. "No, Trevor had to take care of some business out of town."

"That's too bad," Kathryn cooed. "From what I've read, it seems like the two of you are getting close," she said in a conspiratorial tone, like she and Peyton were the best of friends. Carter shot his mother a furious look, but she continued chattering. "I was so sorry to hear of the passing of your mother and stepfather. Such a tragedy."

The comment was so insincere Peyton had the urge to laugh in Kathryn's face. "Oh? I didn't realize you and my mother were close."

Color seeped into Kathryn's face as she laughed nervously. "It's sad to see anyone die that way, regardless of the association."

An awkward moment passed before Kathryn put a proprietary hand on Carter's arm. "Well, it was good to see you, Peyton. But it's time for us to go."

"Not until I escort Peyton back to her seat," Carter said firmly.

Anger splintered over Peyton, giving her a much-needed reminder of how much she detested Carter's glittery world of pretense. And most of all, she detested his horrible mother. "That won't be necessary," she countered frostily. "I can find my own way back."

Carter looked like he might protest, but she forged on, a tight smile on her lips. "Mrs. Webster, it was good to see you again. Carter, thanks for the dances. I'll be sure and tell Art you fulfilled your duty."

She turned on her heel, held her head high, and regally walked away.

CHAPTER 9

athryn was so angry she could claw through metal. "How could you be so stupid?"

"I don't know what you're talking about," Carter said, rubbing his neck.

"You know exactly what I'm talking about," Kathryn countered, speaking in low tones so the other guests wouldn't hear. "Dancing like that with Peyton Kelly."

"You're blowing this way out of proportion. Art Labrum wanted to dance with her, but he can't, so I danced with her on his behalf. It was nothing."

Kathryn didn't know whether to laugh or cry. Carter had such promise, and he was brilliant in so many ways ... but he was a block-head in the one area that mattered the most. Everything they'd worked so hard to achieve was within their grasp, and he was blowing it all on a silly girl. "Don't tell me it was nothing. I saw how you looked at her. Everyone here saw it ... including Millicent," she added in disgust.

"Speaking of which, you said Millicent was looking for me. Where is she?"

Kathryn's lips vanished into a thin line. "She left."

"Then why'd you tell me she was looking for me?"

Was Carter really so obtuse that she had to spell it out for him? "Millicent saw you with Peyton, so she left. And if you have any sense in your thick head, you'll go after her and beg for her forgiveness."

Carter scowled. "Don't count on it, Mother."

She drew herself up to her full height, the lines on her face deepening. "Just what do you mean by that?"

He gave her a hard look. "You and I both know it isn't going to work with Millicent. It's better to come to terms with it now rather than later."

Kathryn's face fell as she gasped, her hand going over her chest. "How can you say that? The two of you are perfect together."

"No, actually, we're not. We have nothing in common. And quite frankly, she bores me stiff."

Kathryn's face drained as she stumbled back.

Carter reached for her arm to steady her. "Are you okay?"

She nodded. "Help me to a chair."

Fitz stepped from the shadows. "Here, allow me," he said, taking her arm. Kathryn leaned on him for support, her lower lip quivering. Fitz looked at Carter. "I'll take it from here."

"I can help," Carter said, worry clouding his features.

Kathryn waved a shaky hand. "I'm okay," she said weakly, turning to Fitz. "Maybe you could take me inside and get me a glass of water?" She eyed Carter, the bite returning to her voice. "If you really want to help, you can make amends with Millicent. Fitz, let's go," she snapped.

Fitz nodded and steered her toward the door. When they stepped inside, Kathryn let go of Fitz's arm and stood up straight.

Fitz chuckled. "Just as I thought. You know, there are easier ways to fix this situation without you being reduced to pandering to your son. Just say the word, and I'll take care of the whole thing."

Fire licked through her eyes. "First of all, I don't appreciate being accused of pandering. And secondly, I've got the situation under control."

He looked doubtful.

"*If* and *when* I need your help, I will most certainly let you know," she said testily.

He smiled, not in the least affected by her outburst. "Just remember ... when you exhaust your resources, I'll be here to help."

～

THE SUN SHONE BRIGHTLY OVERHEAD, a warm breeze blowing. Peyton was in a park on a merry-go-round and Carter was spinning her. She held on, laughing, but then he spun her faster. "Stop," she yelled, but he only smiled and kept spinning her faster and faster. Her hands started to slip as tears slid from her eyes. "Carter! Please. It's too fast. I can't hold on—"

A loud *bam* shattered the stillness of the night as Peyton shot up in bed. Her heart was beating shallow and fast, and it was difficult to get a good breath. She forced herself to calm down, pushing back the covers. It was a stupid dream!

No sooner had her feet touched the ground when she jerked at the sound of a door slamming shut. Fear iced over her as she reached for her phone and got out bed. Then she heard the soft crying. She froze, listening. This time, she heard laughter. It sounded just like her mother. Tears sprang to her eyes as she gasped, not believing what she was hearing. Somehow, she made her way to the wall and flipped on the light. "Who's there?" she demanded.

Silence.

A paralyzing fear came over her. But she couldn't just stand here. Should she call the police? And tell them what, that she'd heard her dead mother's laughter? A hysterical laugh bubbled in her throat. She didn't believe in ghosts.

Heart pounding, she stepped into the hall and flipped on the light. From what she could tell, the sound had come from the attic. But there was no way she was going up there in the dark ... by herself. She walked down the curved staircase and flipped on all the lights in the main room. Everything looked untouched.

Still trembling, Peyton rummaged through a box of kitchen items shoved against the wall of the living room and pulled out a long kitchen knife. It wasn't the best weapon, but it was all she had.

She grabbed a bottle of water from the mini-fridge and sat on the edge of the sofa, placing the knife beside her. Her heart was still hammering in her chest, and she was bathed in sticky sweat. What in the heck was happening? Was there a ghost in the house? No, that was impossible. Was someone trying to scare her? She shuddered. The thought of someone in the house was almost scarier than the prospect of a ghost.

Tomorrow morning she would search the attic. And she needed to talk to Karen Sandburg to find out what she'd seen. She reached for a blanket as she scooted back on the sofa. She took a sip of the water and placed the bottle on the nearby table. Then she clutched the knife, holding it in one hand and her phone in the other. She sat there, her eyes darting around the room, waiting for something to happen. Finally, she drifted off into an uneasy sleep.

The next morning she returned to her bedroom and saw her mother's opal ring on the dresser. Very odd. As far as Peyton knew, there was nothing significant about the ring. Only that it should've been packed away with the rest of her mother's belongings. How in the heck had it ended up on the dresser?

PEYTON APPLIED the grout in jerky movements, keeping her eyes trained to the ceramic tile pieces rather than Carter. But she felt his probing eyes surveying her.

"What?"

"Nothing." A hint of a smile touched his lips. "Just wondering why you're starting at the bottom of the shower when we still haven't done that section at the top."

She looked to where he was pointing. *Crap!* She'd been so consumed by the strangeness of the night before that she'd forgotten about the section above the decorative pieces. She let out a long sigh.

"At this point, there's nothing we can do except wait until the shower floor dries before we finish the upper section."

He nodded. "Well, at least let me help you with the floor."

She shrugged. "Thanks." Lack of sleep and worry were wearing on her. She couldn't sleep after she saw her mother's ring on the dresser, but nothing was amiss in the attic. It looked the same as it had the day she'd moved into the bed and breakfast.

Carter studied her. "Are you okay? You look a little tired this morning."

She turned to him. "Tell me the truth—are you the one who's been leaving breakfast items on my porch?" Every other morning, she'd eaten them. But this morning, she threw the pastry in the trash. For all she knew, the items could be laced with something. Well, maybe not. If they had been, it would have affected her by now. But still, it couldn't hurt to be safe. "Is it you?"

"What do you think?"

"Just tell me, okay?"

He touched her arm. "Hey, what's going on?"

"I think someone was in my house last night." Saying the words aloud made it seem a thousand times worse.

"What?"

"I heard a noise in the attic." She didn't tell him about the crying, laughter, or the ring, for fear he'd think she was crazy. "I didn't dare check it until this morning, but everything seems normal ... from what I can tell."

"Did you call the police?"

"No. I probably should have. But I was sound asleep when I heard the noise. It woke me up ..." The words dribbled off. She knew she wasn't making sense, but she couldn't tell him the full story.

"You should've called me. I would've come over."

"It was probably the wind. I don't want to make a mountain out of a molehill, know what I mean?"

His eyes searched hers. "Promise you'll call me if anything like that happens again."

She nodded.

"I mean it. Call me, okay?"

"Okay."

"It's an old house, and I'm sure there are lots of strange sounds. It's probably nothing."

"I'm sure you're right," she mumbled, not wanting to discuss it any further.

"And yes, I've been leaving food on your front porch. I was trying to help, not scare you to death." He shook his head. "I'm sorry I added to the stress."

"It has helped. I really appreciate it." Without thinking, she touched his arm. Their eyes met as the moment slowed. And at that moment, she really wanted to kiss him. Oh no! What was she doing? It was so easy to fall back into old habits with Carter. But that would be a mistake. As nonchalantly as she could, she removed her hand.

"I had fun dancing with you the other night." Carter flashed his trademark crooked smile. "I'm just sorry that we got interrupted."

Still reeling from the intense attraction she felt for him, she tried to say something to put distance between them. "Well, like you said—you fulfilled your duty to Art."

Amusement sparked his eyes. "Who do you think prompted Art to make a big deal about dancing in the first place?"

She coughed. "Are you saying the whole thing was a setup?" It'd been easier to believe Carter danced with her out of duty. Now she wasn't sure what to think.

"Those are your words, not mine."

There was no winning an argument with Carter. "Well, if your mother had anything to do with it, she would've had me thrown out on my ear."

He laughed. "Yes, you're probably right. You're not exactly my mother's favorite person," he said matter-of-factly.

Her forehead creased. "Yeah, well, the feeling's mutual. I'll bet she just loves Millicent." She didn't try to hide her resentment.

"As far as my mother's concerned, Millicent's the perfect woman for me."

"Well, congratulations," she said darkly. "It seems like everything's working out splendidly for you."

He scrunched his nose. "Not really. Millicent and I are through."

"Oh, I'm sorry," she said automatically.

"I'm not."

His intense eyes had a magnetic quality that drew her in. "Really?"

"Really." The slightest hint of a smile touched his features. "Yeah, I mean, a guy can only listen so long to a girl drone on about clothes, makeup, and every insignificant detail about the social framework of Sonoma Valley."

"Come on," she teased, "you know you love talking about eye shadow and lipstick."

He shuddered. "Yeah, right."

A comfortable silence settled between them as they turned their attention back to the grout.

"There is one thing I would like to talk about," he said casually.

"Oh, yeah? What's that?"

"What's the story between you and Trevor?"

"We have a show together. What more is there to know?" she said casually.

He gave her a probing look. "I told you about Millicent. The least you can do is give it to me straight." He nudged her with his elbow. "You know, friend-to-friend?"

She toppled sideways, then shoved him. "Stop. You're getting me off balance."

His eyes lit with mischief. "That was the intent."

Darn those butterflies fluttering in her breast! How was it possible for a guy to be so irritating and sexy at the same time?

An easy smile spread over his lips. "Come on, Peyton. You owe me that much."

She sighed. "Trevor and I are just friends."

He gave her a sidelong glance. "I could've sworn I read somewhere the two of you were an item."

"Yeah, most of that's fabricated for publicity." The relief that swelled over Carter's face cut her to the quick, making her feel like she'd tossed Trevor under the bus. "Trevor would like for us to be more than friends, though," she blurted.

He stopped working, his eyes penetrating hers. "And what do you want?"

What did she want? Even as she asked herself the question, her mind screamed it. *You!* Had she really just thought that? Yes, unfortunately she had. It was hard to admit, but it was a painful truth. Despite everything, a part of her still wanted Carter. "I-I'm not sure," she said, looking away.

He let out a breath. "Well, look on the bright side. You don't have to make a decision today. In fact, you don't have to make a decision tomorrow ... or the next day either. Just take it one step at a time. When the time's right, you'll know."

She chuckled. "Thank you, Dr. Phil, for those wise words of wisdom. I'll be sure to keep them in mind."

His eyes caressed hers. "Yes, please do." He touched her hair.

Her breath caught as her heart began to pound. They were so close, she could smell peppermint on his breath, catch the tiny gold flecks in his eyes, see the faint dusting of freckles over his nose.

He backed away, holding up his hand. "You had grout in your hair. Sorry."

"Oh, thanks," she said, disappointed he'd not kissed her. Then again, she probably would've slapped him if he had. She jutted out her chin. Yes, she most definitely would've slapped him! Where were these idiotic thoughts coming from?

"Hey, I was thinking ... would you like to have dinner with me tonight?"

Peyton's first reaction was *no*, but then she saw his eyes shift slightly, the way they did when he was nervous. It was not often she caught a glimpse of Carter's vulnerable side. And it was surprisingly endearing.

His words spilled out between them. "I mean, I figured it would be nice for us to go ... since you don't have a kitchen."

"I would like that," she said, almost before she realized what she was saying.

He rewarded her with a brilliant smile that melted her heart. "Fantastic. It's a date."

She frowned. "A date?"

"A figure of speech," he said calmly. "We're just two old friends having dinner." His eyes searched hers. "Okay?"

"Okay. But as friends," she added firmly.

He nodded. "So, friend, should I pick you up at seven?"

"Seven sounds good."

CHAPTER 10

*P*eyton applied strokes of blush, followed by mascara, and finally, a shimmery, soft bare lipstick. She fluffed her hair and did a final check of her reflection in the mirror. She'd chosen a red sweater, leggings, her favorite boots, and gold hoop earrings. A feverish excitement was building inside her, and she kept waffling back and forth between her desire to go to dinner with Carter and the need to protect her herself from getting hurt by him. It was no big deal. They were simply having dinner as friends. That was all.

Right?

She looked in the mirror and frowned. Even her reflection didn't believe her.

Carter Webster was just as much her weak spot now as he'd ever been. And it didn't help that he was being so stinking nice to her. It still boggled her mind that he'd been bringing her breakfast every morning. Working with him on Art's job was an unexpectedly pleasant experience. It was hard to believe he was the same callous, unfeeling jerk who had broken her heart. It was like he was two different people. A part of her wondered if she should just bite the bullet and confront him about all that had happened the night of their pre-wedding party so she could begin anew. Maybe even with Trevor.

After all, she was super fond of him, although there were no fireworks in their relationship. Trevor was stable—the kind of guy she could count on. And that spoke volumes. Fireworks were way overrated ... weren't they?

She looked at her phone. It was five minutes 'til seven. Carter was punctual to the minute. They'd not talked about where they were going to dinner. She briefly wondered if she might be underdressed, but sloughed off the thought. They were just friends, so of course it didn't matter how she was dressed. She quickly put her makeup and hair products away and tidied up the sink vanity.

Then she heard something. The fears from the night before came rushing back with a vengeance as she went still, craning her ears. The house had felt so bright and cheerful when she'd come home this afternoon that she'd almost convinced herself the events from the night before had stemmed from her imagination and Courtney's stories. But there it was again ... a slight cracking sound. She was wide awake now and certainly not imagining things.

Peyton's skin crawled as she whipped around. "Who's there?" Carefully, she opened the bathroom door, holding her breath. The bedroom was clear. She looked under the bed and checked the closet for good measure. Her pulse increased as she left the bedroom and eased down the hall, where she stopped in her tracks, straining to hear.

Another creaking sound!

Was it the wind? She was grateful to be going out with Carter tonight so she wouldn't have to spend the evening alone. Of course, she still had to come back here to sleep. At this point, she didn't know how in the world she was going to make herself do it.

This morning, faced with the daunting task of checking the attic, she'd been tempted to call Trevor and ask him to come back early, but decided against it. He was knee-deep in his renovation project. And the last few conversations they had were strained. Furthermore, she didn't want Trevor asking questions about Carter. If Trevor knew she was having dinner with Carter, he'd be so ticked he might not return.

Another creak nearly sent her jumping out of her skin, and she had the urge to flee. But to where? She stood paralyzed, unsure what to do. And then she heard the doorbell. The relief that flooded her was nearly palpable. Her knees went weak as she rushed down the staircase and flung open the door, nearly bounding into Carter's arms.

"Hey," she said breathlessly. "I'm so glad you're here."

He chuckled. "Thanks." Then he got a good look at her face. "What's wrong? You're pale as a ghost."

Without warning, tears pooled in her eyes. "I was getting ready, and I heard something. This time, I know I didn't imagine it." Her voice caught. "I think someone's in the house. Should we call the police?" she whispered.

He stepped inside and closed the door. "Let's take things one step at a time. What did you hear?"

"A creaking noise."

"It's windy outside. Do you think maybe a branch is rubbing against a window?"

She pushed her hair back, a futile frustration boiling inside her. "I don't know ... maybe."

There was a long pause as he silently assessed her. "Okay, I'll check the entire house."

She clutched his arm. "But if someone's here, they could attack you. Maybe I should get a knife ... or something."

He gave her a funny look. "All this for a creaking noise? What's going on, Peyton?"

Should she tell him what really happened the night before? It was all so bizarre. He would think she was losing her mind. Then again, she needed to tell someone, and Carter seemed genuinely concerned. "I promise, I'll tell you everything," she said quietly, "but first we need to check the house."

She rushed to the silverware box and retrieved the same kitchen knife from the night before.

Carter's eyes widened, and he let out a nervous laugh. "Whoa, that's a little extreme."

Her jaw clenched. "You won't think so when I tell you everything."

Cautiously, he stepped up to her and took the knife from her hands. "Maybe I should hold on to this."

"Suit yourself. So long as one of us has it." Her eyes narrowed as she raised her voice to the empty air. "I don't know what's going on here, but mark my words, I'm going to get to the bottom of it."

~

IT TOOK effort for Carter to keep his expression neutral while Peyton told him the story, when what he really wanted to do was jump up and yell, *Are you crazy?*

"You don't believe me," Peyton said flatly, hurt emanating from her dark eyes.

Carter rubbed a hand across his forehead. "I didn't say that. I'm just trying to process it, that's all."

Peyton's lips drew into a tight line as she sat back in her seat and clamped her arms over her chest. "Don't you dare lie to me, Carter Webster. I know you don't believe me. I can see it in your eyes."

"I'm trying to believe you, but it's so ..."

She arched an eyebrow. "Bizarre? Far-fetched?" She began tapping her fingers on her arm. "Trust me, I know."

They were sitting at a booth, tucked in the corner of one of the two restaurants owned by Carter and his mother. Having feasted on roast duck, tri-tip, roasted potatoes, a crisp salad with tangy blue cheese dressing, and crusty bread, the conversation shifted to the serious topic of the bed and breakfast. Before leaving for the restaurant, Carter and Peyton searched the house from top to bottom and found nothing out of the ordinary. This seemed to upset Peyton more than if they'd found something or someone.

Carter looked across the table at Peyton. The soft candlelight flickering against her face emphasized her delicate cheekbones. He could get lost in the mystery of her expressive chocolate eyes. Her exquisite lips were set in a defiant stance, daring him to disagree with her. He was reminded again of how Peyton was a tantalizing mixture of tenderness and strength. He longed to pull her into his arms and soothe the tension from her face. But everything she was telling him was so hard to swallow. The crying in the middle of the night. Her mother's laughter … and the ring?

Peyton was a straight-shooter from the word *go*, but grief did strange things to people. Was it possible she'd imagined it all? Maybe coming home had been too much for her. Running off the way she had pointed to erratic behavior, and Peyton's mother had been eccentric. Maybe Peyton had inherited a touch of the crazy too. After all, it had been years since he and Peyton had been around each other. He couldn't assume she was the same person he'd known before. The chilling thoughts caused a knot to form in his stomach.

"I don't believe in ghosts, and I'm not crazy, if that's what you're thinking," Peyton said, looking him in the eye.

She'd always had the uncanny ability to read his thoughts. He chuckled inwardly, feeling a measure of relief. At least that was one way she hadn't changed. "Okay, let's take this a step at a time … ruling out the ghost and your imagination. Karen Sandburg claims she heard crying and saw a woman rounding the corner. Have you spoken to her?"

"Not yet, but I'm going to call her first thing in the morning."

"I'd like to go with you when you visit her."

"Of course." She blew out a breath. "Look, I know how crazy this sounds. All I can think is that someone's trying to scare me away."

"Who would want to do that?"

She let out a harsh chuckle. "Well, you, for starters."

He rocked back. "Surely, you don't think I would do something like that?" It stung to know she thought so little of him.

She eyed him for a long moment. "No, I don't think it's you."

He rolled his eyes. "I can assure you, it's not."

"What about your mother?"

"Are you serious?" He laughed. "My mother's a lot of things, but I can't picture her skulking around in your attic, pretending to be a ghost."

"You never know. She's never had my best interest at heart. She never wanted us to get together in the first place, and now that I'm back and the two of us are spending time together and getting close again—" Peyton stopped, her eyes growing large, like she just realized what she said.

The hope that kindled in Carter's chest surprised him. He cocked his head, a smile tugging at his lips. "Surely you're not suggesting the two of us could be anything other than friends?"

Her face turned scarlet. "Absolutely not."

It was fun watching Peyton squirm. Was it possible she still had feelings for him? The way she'd looked at him earlier today, when they were working on the shower floor, made him wonder. "I'm just kidding," Carter said before she got too uncomfortable. He knew from experience that if he pushed her too far, she would storm out of the restaurant. He was enjoying spending time with Peyton and wanted the evening to last as long as possible.

She relaxed a fraction. "Other than you and your mother, I can't think of anyone who would want me out of the bed and breakfast."

He sidestepped the accusation in her voice. "What about Andrea?"

Peyton thought for a minute. "No, she hates the bed and breakfast and was all too happy to sell her half to you. She wasn't even willing to help me pack up my mother and Harold's things."

"Until we figure out what's going on, you don't need to be there alone."

"Where else would I stay? Unlike you, I don't have a five-star-resort at my disposal."

He laughed, loving Peyton's fiery temperament. "I guess it's true what they say."

"What?"

He cast an appraising eye over her. "Dynamite really does come in small packages."

"Oh, shut up," she teased as her lips twitched.

"Anyway, as I was saying ..." His eyebrow shot up. "... before I was so rudely interrupted ... it's not a good idea for you to stay there alone." He paused. "I'm moving in."

Her jaw dropped. "What? No, you can't."

"There's plenty of room. And it's half mine. So you see, there's nothing you can do to stop me."

Time seemed to stand still as she sized him up. "Okay," she finally said, her eyes growing tender. "Thank you. For all your tough talk about owning half the place, I know it's a headache for you to move in, especially considering there's no kitchen. But I really appreciate it. And I would feel much safer with you there."

Carter was unprepared for the wave of emotion that tumbled over him as he swallowed. "You're welcome," he said gruffly, taking a drink from his glass.

Peyton sighed. "One good turn deserves another." She began fidgeting with her napkin. "Look, I know we agreed not to discuss the fate of the bed and breakfast until after we finish Art's job, but I've been thinking a lot about it. What if we hire an arbitrator? We'll each tell him our side of the story and then abide by his decision." She gave him a tentative look. "What do you think?"

"Do you have someone in mind?"

"Yes." Quickly, she told him about Courtney's uncle. "I don't even know if he'll agree to take us on as clients, but I can check."

An arbitrator sounded like a viable solution. Although, Carter was so stoked by the prospect of staying at the bed and breakfast with Peyton he could think of little else. "Sure, that sounds good."

She nodded. "I'll see what I can set up."

The waitress returned. "Would you like to order dessert?"

Carter looked at Peyton. "The double fudge cake is outstanding."

"That sounds good, but I can only eat a couple of bites. I'm stuffed."

"We'll order one and share," Carter said.

CHAPTER 11

*P*eyton deposited her purse on the couch and turned to Carter. "There's bottled water in the mini-fridge and snacks in the pie safe." She'd created a makeshift station in the living room so she could at least make sandwiches and heat food in the microwave. Now that Peyton and Carter were here alone ... together ... in this big house ... she wasn't quite sure how to act. It was one thing to have him stop by, but quite another to know he was staying here with her. A mixture of excitement and trepidation battled in her stomach, and her voice sounded unnaturally loud in her ears. "Do you need to run to your place and grab some clothes?" Her eyes flickered over him. "I'm afraid I don't have anything that'll fit you."

He grinned, seeming to pick up on her discomfort. "I think I'll be okay for tonight. I'll get my stuff tomorrow."

She let out a derisive chuckle. "I'd like to be a fly on the wall when you tell your mother you're staying here."

His brows creased. "Hey, now. Quit bagging on my mother."

"I'm not! Just making a statement."

He gave her a censured look. "My mother hasn't had the easiest time of it since you've been gone."

She pulled a face. "What, did her hairstylist move to another state?"

He hesitated. "No, she has leukemia."

Peyton's jaw dropped. "Are you serious?"

He nodded.

She wanted to crawl under the rug. "I-I'm sorry. I didn't know."

"It's okay." He plopped down on the sofa and propped his feet on the nearby ottoman.

Peyton sat down beside him, trying to think of something to say that wouldn't sound insincere or unfeeling. She didn't wish leukemia on anyone, not even Kathryn Webster. "So, is your mother okay?"

"More or less. As far as leukemia goes, she's lucky. She has chronic lymphocytic leukemia, meaning her leukemia is slowly progressing. Something she can live with. ... Stress and exhaustion exacerbate her symptoms, so she has to be careful."

"Is she undergoing treatment?"

"In the beginning, she did a combo of chemotherapy and radiation, but the disease is now stable."

She clasped her hands tightly in her lap. "I'm sorry for what I said about her hairstylist. That was uncalled for."

He waved her apology away. "No worries."

Peyton scrunched her nose. "Why does your mother hate me so much?"

"Hate's a rather strong word," he countered.

"Call it what you will. The question is, *why*?"

He shifted in his seat. "How am I supposed to know what's in her head?"

"Oh, no. You're not getting out of this one. Tell me," she pressed.

He let out a long sigh. "My mother's a complicated woman. She has such high aspirations for me. At one time, she wanted me to go into politics."

She pursed her lips. "Hmm ... I can see that. You're a whiz at negotiations, and no one can win an argument against you."

He was amused. "Really?"

"Yeah, really. You'd make a pretty good politician."

He winced. "No, thank you. I'll stick to running the businesses. Speaking of which, things are crazy at the vineyards right now during crush. As much as I hate to do it, I'm going to have to put off Art's job this coming week and let you handle the bulk of it."

"Oh, I see how it is," she quipped, even though she understood. In fact, he'd spent so much time on Art's project, she was beginning to wonder if he actually worked in the Webster *empire* or was merely a figurehead. It was reassuring to know he was a viable part of the businesses—that he was making a valuable contribution to the community. She stopped, chuckling inwardly. *As if any of it mattered to her.* Once they were finished with Art's project and when the ownership question of the bed and breakfast was settled, she and Carter would part ways. A sense of melancholy covered her, and she realized with a jolt that she was enjoying spending time with Carter. In many ways, some sleeping part of her was awakening, allowing her to fully live again. Geez! Had she really just thought that? Talk about dangerous territory! She brushed aside the thoughts, going back to their earlier conversation. "You still didn't answer my question."

A quizzical look came over him, and he was the picture of innocence. "What question?"

She shoved him. "You know what question. Why your mother doesn't like me?"

"Okay. First of all, it's not you personally she doesn't like."

She frowned. "Why does everyone say that? *It's not you personally,*" she mimicked. "It certainly feels personal."

"Aside from the obvious part about me growing up rich and you poor, which unfortunately does matter to her, you don't fit into a neat little box." His eyes took on a peculiar glow as he continued. "You're headstrong, spontaneous, not confined by convention. And you can't be controlled by anyone, least of all my mother."

The air around them stilled as she looked him in the eye. "Is that such a bad thing?"

A smile spread over his lips, casting a mesmerizing light over his features. Her eyes traced his jawbone, and she longed to run her finger along his layer of stubble as she had so many times before. Every angle and curve of his face was permanently etched in her memory.

"No, those are the very things I love about you," Carter said softly. His eyes caressed hers, reaching through her carefully crafted armor and into her soul.

Peyton's breath hitched as she caught the meaning of his words. He was speaking in present tense, not past. She clenched her fist so hard that her nails dug into her palm. She could almost imagine the years they'd spent apart peeling away like insignificant flecks of old paint to reveal the beautiful wood below. Here, in this moment, they were as they'd been before. No barriers. No restrictions. Only a glorious, all-consuming love that was as turbulent as it was fulfilling. Without warning, tears rushed to her eyes, and she blinked rapidly to keep them at bay.

Carter scooted closer and stroked her hair. "Did I say something wrong?"

A smile escaped her lips. "No, as usual, you said everything right." The words were an admission she was sure to regret, but she couldn't seem to summon the willpower to stop.

Longing stirred in his eyes, deepened them to a smoldering gray as he leaned in. "Peyton," he uttered.

A quiver of urgency raced through Peyton as she parted her lips, her pulse spiking. A warning bell sounded in her head, but she silenced it. She wanted this right now, more than she wanted air.

Her phone buzzed, breaking the spell as she backed away. "I need to get that," she said regretfully.

Carter nodded, disappointed.

She pulled the phone from her purse and answered it. "Trevor … hey …" She caught the frustrated look on Carter's face as she stood and walked to the far corner of the room. "What's up?"

THE FOLLOWING MORNING, Peyton found a pastry and a container of juice outside her bedroom door, along with a note from Carter saying he would be tied up at the vineyards for the bulk of the day but would catch up with her in the evening for dinner. She felt herself smile as she traced over his familiar handwriting with her finger. Even as she drifted off to sleep the night before, she kept thinking about that moment when they'd almost kissed. She kept trying to convince herself that Trevor's phone call had been a welcome interruption, saving her from making a huge mistake. But she couldn't deny she was disappointed. A large part of her wanted to kiss Carter again, see if kissing him would be as good as she remembered. Judging by the attraction that sparked like a Roman candle every time she came near him, it would.

She unwrapped the pastry and took a large bite, savoring the taste of the flaky crust against the tart strawberry filling. If she hadn't seen and heard all those things the night of their pre-wedding party, Carter would be the perfect man. She'd finally had a good night's sleep, knowing he was in the room next door. And nothing strange had happened. No noises ... nothing. It would seem Carter's presence was a deterrent for whatever weirdness was taking place. Only time would tell for sure.

Maybe she should start judging Carter by his present acts rather than the man he was in the past. After all, it had been quite some time since he'd broken her heart. She let out a long sigh. There was still the fate of the bed and breakfast looming over them. She needed to call Courtney's uncle to see if he would mediate their case and Karen Sandburg to see if she and Carter could pay her a visit.

Ten minutes later, she'd managed to set up an appointment for the end of the week with Curtis Dunkin, the arbitrator. Karen didn't answer, so she left a voicemail asking her to return the call. Then she went out the door and headed to Art's house.

THE FIRST THING Peyton noticed when she stepped into Art's home was the classical music playing in the background. "Hello," she called, walking through the foyer into the living room. She found Art sitting in his recliner, a book spread over his lap, his fingers pressing against the pages—reading.

He looked past her. "Come in."

"Good morning," Peyton said heartily. She strode across the room and gave him a hug. "I'm afraid it's just me today. Carter has lots of work to catch up on at the vineyard."

A smile touched his lips as he tilted his head, looking thoughtful. "Yes, crush is a busy time of year. Carter's pulling double duty with the vineyards and wineries. In today's world, most vineyards and wineries have separate owners. It's rare to find a family or company that owns both. But it makes sense. The best way to ensure that you have quality grapes is to grow them yourself. Of course, so much goes into that aspect of it, it even has its own name. Viticulture involves the science of the various stages that go into grape growing and harvesting. It's really quite fascinating when you realize how delicate and integral the processes are." He paused, shaking his head. "Listen to me, droning on. Have a seat. It's not often we get a chance to talk."

Peyton was itching to get to work, but it was obvious Art was craving company. She sat down on the sofa across from him.

Art placed his book on the nearby table. "So, how have you been?"

"Good." Silence stretched between them, and she could tell he was waiting for more. She scrambled for something to add. She didn't want to mention her plans for renovating the bed and breakfast, because that would lead to her putting those on hold to take care of his project. Nor did she dare admit she'd been hearing weird noises. And she certainly couldn't talk about her growing attraction to Carter. "It's sometimes strange being in such a large house by myself. Carter was kind enough to move into one of the rooms so I won't be alone."

He raised an eyebrow, looking impressed. "That's nice." Long pause. "It can't be easy for you to be there without your mother. I know you miss her very much."

Peyton gulped, shocked at how quickly Art had skipped the preliminaries and gone to the heart of the matter. There was something so pure and sincere about the way he voiced the words. "Yes," she croaked, not trying to hide the hot tears that spilled down her cheeks. For the first time, she was glad Art couldn't see. She wiped them away with the heels of her palms. "It's been tough. The memories of her are everywhere." Her voice quivered. "It's painful. And yet, I can't bear the thought of the house not being there."

He nodded. "That's why you feel the need to restore the home—so you can fix that broken part of yourself."

The comment was like a blow to the gut, catching her completely off guard. Was she broken? Sure, she was struggling, but who wouldn't be under the circumstances? She sucked in a breath. "I—I haven't really thought about it that way." Okay, now she was super ready to end this little convo. Maybe Art had missed his calling. He should've been a psychologist.

"Sometimes you have to break something apart to make it stronger and better. The Lord doesn't give us trials to break us, but to strengthen us."

It was an interesting prospect. One she would have to think about … some other time. It was on the tip of her tongue to tell him she was on a tight schedule, but she remained quiet as he continued, his voice contemplative.

"When I first lost my sight, I was angry at the world … but mostly I was angry at God. I thought, *Why me?* I'd been a good person. Spent my life teaching and helping others. It seemed so unfair."

"I can only imagine how you must've felt." She'd experienced similar feelings, growing up in the home of an alcoholic. And they were magnified a hundredfold when her mother was taken from her … through the careless actions of the very person who'd caused her so much grief.

"One particular day, I was low." Art hesitated, and a shudder seemed to ripple through him. "So low I didn't know if I could go on." He drew in a breath. "But then there was a knock at the door. I didn't answer it, but the person kept knocking. Or rather pounding. By this point, I was perturbed. I wasn't even dressed. I managed to throw on a robe as I stumbled to the door. I flung it open, glaring at the offender, even though I couldn't see a thing. Who do you think was there?"

Sensing it was a rhetorical question, Peyton remained silent.

Art grinned. "Carter. 'Good morning,' he said cheerfully, pushing past me into the house. 'I've come to take you to breakfast. So you'd better get dressed.'"

Peyton was surprised. "What did you do?"

He shook his head. "I blustered around a bit, mumbling a few unsavory words under my breath. But in the end, Carter left me no choice. I got dressed, and we went to breakfast. Carter's been coming by at least once a week ever since." He looked her direction, and she had the impression his soul was seeing hers. "Are you the praying type, Peyton?"

"Yes, I am." She felt guilty for answering in the affirmative because she hadn't done much praying lately. But she was still a firm believer in prayer.

"I wasn't … until I lost my sight. I always thought I was too educated for religion. That it was a crutch for the weak-minded." He chuckled ruefully. "It's ironic that it took the darkness to help me come into the light. One thing I've come to learn is that prayer is real, and we have a loving Heavenly Father who's aware of our deepest hurts and most fervent desires. He knows our hearts, and He desires to bless us. But He often does so through other people. Carter was the answer to the prayer my lips had failed to utter."

The words burned into Peyton's heart. If anyone else were speaking about such topics, she might've dismissed them, thinking they were fanciful or preachy. But knowing all Art had been through … hearing the gratitude he expressed over simple things was touching.

"And do you know what Carter said when I asked him why he chose that particular day to drop by and invite me to breakfast?" He chuckled, not waiting for her to answer. "Carter said, 'I was hungry, and thought you might be too.'"

Peyton laughed despite herself. "Sounds like him."

"Carter reminds me a lot of his dad. Did you know Bradley?"

"No, he passed away before Carter and I really knew each other." She tried to remember. "What did he die of?"

"A brain hemorrhage. He fell at one of the wineries and hit his head. It was tragic—a freak accident. Anyway, Bradley was always helping the community. When the football boosters needed uniforms, Bradley was the first one to step up to the plate. Bradley built the new gym and field house. He was very generous that way. Whenever he saw a need, he jumped to help."

"Carter's been good to me, too, since I've been back," she admitted. "He's been leaving me breakfast every morning."

He shook his head. "Carter and his breakfast. You know ..." He paused midsentence, causing Peyton to lean forward, intent on hearing the rest. "He cares a great deal for you."

"Really?"

Art laughed. "Don't sound so surprised."

"After what happened between us ..." Her voice faded into the stuffy air. Some things were too personal to share, even with Art.

Art's expression was kind and patient, like he was giving Peyton ample space to come to terms with her issues. He was among the lucky few who are impervious to the hustle and bustle of everyday life. His world was here, amidst his treasured books, soothing music, and memories. It wasn't a bad way to live, Peyton decided.

Art's voice had a lyrical quality as he began quoting, "'In the summer of youth, strands of love are woven effortlessly like the silken threads of a spider web. It is not until later—when the fading dusk quietly casts her lengthening shadows—that those delicate strands become bonds of steel which buoy us up and lend support in the wintertime of our lives.'"

She titled her head, searching her memory. "I haven't heard that one before. Did you write it?"

"No, it was written by a close friend. It's one of my favorites ... simple, yet profound." He brought his hands together, forming a steeple with his fingers. "Regardless of what happened between you and Carter, I know the two of you can work it out."

"Yeah, I'm not so sure."

"Coming back here has been good for you, Peyton."

"I suppose that remains to be seen," she said stiffly, feeling emotionally drained. She scooted to the edge of her seat. "If you don't mind, I need to get to work."

"Yes, of course. There is just one more question I want to ask."

"Okay," she said warily.

"When you renovate a home, what is the first step?"

She had no clue where this was going. "The design."

He waved a hand. "Yes, after the design … when you start the actual project."

"I'm not sure what you mean."

He held up a finger. "You tear out the old."

"Yes, that's correct."

"And then you rebuild the new … layer upon layer. Am I right?"

She got the feeling she was once again a student in his classroom. "Yes."

He gave her a wise smile. "Had you not come back here, you would never have been whole. You have spent the last few years trying to rebuild, but you haven't dealt with the past. Do so, and the healing will come."

She bit down on her lower lips, clamping her arms tightly over her chest.

"You may find this surprising, but when I was your teacher, I used to watch you and Carter. I would think to myself, 'Those two have a magic that most people can only dream of.'"

Tears brimmed in Peyton's eyes.

"And even though my sight has left me …" He placed a hand over his heart. "…whenever I'm around you both, I can still feel that same magic in here." He paused. "Do yourself a favor—talk to Carter … soon. For not a one of us is guaranteed a tomorrow."

CHAPTER 12

As Peyton walked across the front yard of her house, she stopped and did a double take. There was a new tire swing hanging on the lowest branch of the large oak tree. All throughout her growing-up years, the tire swing had been a fixture, and she was sad when she returned after her mother's death to find it gone. But there it was, plain as day. She wasn't sure if she should be glad or worried.

Her phone buzzed. She reached in her purse and retrieved it. She didn't recognize the number, but it was a Cloverdale area code. "Hello."

"Hi, Peyton. This is Karen Sandburg, returning your call."

"Hey, Karen. The reason I called is because I wanted to talk to you about what you saw and heard when you were in my house packing up my mother and Harold's belongings."

Long pause.

"Hello? Karen, are you there?"

"Yes," came the curt reply.

"Is there a good time for me to stop by? I really need to know what you saw. It's important," she added.

"Okay," Karen relented. "How about tomorrow afternoon at three?"

"That works for me." Peyton wasn't sure if Carter would be able to go with her, since he was slammed with work. But the sooner she got to the bottom of that situation, the better. "I'll see you tomorrow." As she ended the call, Courtney pulled into the driveway.

"Hey," Courtney said, giving her a hug. "How are things?"

"Good." She pointed. "This may seem like a strange question, but do you remember that tire swing being there before?"

"I don't know. Why?"

"Just curious." Peyton walked over, inspecting it. The tire was shiny and the rope new.

Courtney gave her a funny look. "What's going on?"

"Nothing."

"Really?" She raised an eyebrow.

Peyton forced a smile. "Really." Even though Courtney was a good friend, Peyton wasn't comfortable sharing the strange happenings at the bed and breakfast. At least not until she spoke to Karen Sandburg. Courtney was already superstitious about haunted houses; there was no sense in adding fuel to that fire.

"Okay," Courtney said. "I thought I'd stop by and see if you want to go to dinner and a movie."

Peyton wrinkled her nose. "Ooh, sorry, I wish could. But I can't."

She put a hand on her hip. "You have other plans?"

"Sort of."

Courtney waved a hand. "Spill it."

Peyton sighed. She might as well tell Courtney now, because she would find out soon enough anyway. "Carter's moving in."

Her jaw dropped. "What?"

"He was worried about me being here alone, so he offered to move in." She flushed. "Separate bedrooms, of course."

"When did this happen?"

"Last night."

"Oh my gosh!" Courtney's eyes danced. "Does Trevor know?"

"No, I haven't had a chance to tell him."

Courtney laughed. "I'll bet you haven't." She gave Peyton a sly look. "So, I take it things are going well with you and Carter? Obviously."

"Yeah, we're getting along okay."

Courtney motioned with her eyes. "What about the bed and breakfast? Any decision on that?"

"No, but I contacted your uncle, and he's agreed to meet with Carter and me this coming Thursday."

"Good, I'm glad he was able to take your case."

"I think it helped that I told him I was your friend."

"Yeah ... maybe." Courtney sighed loudly, envy sparking in her eyes. "I can't believe you have two gorgeous guys falling over you."

Peyton rolled her eyes. "Carter's hardly falling over me. He's simply trying to help."

"Yeah ... sure. And I'm Mother Teresa. I guess I'll have to go to the movies by myself," she pouted.

"Well, would you like to at least come in and hang out for a while? I have a few bottles of Perrier chilling in the mini-fridge."

"Thanks, but I'd like to grab something to eat before the movie starts."

"Let's plan ahead, and I'll go with you next time."

"Sounds good." Her eyes took on a devilish glint. "Be sure and tell Carter I said hello," she chimed.

"I will," Peyton said, matching her singsong tone.

Courtney gave her a quick hug. "See ya."

"Bye."

PEYTON WAS ON HER LAPTOP, getting caught up on email, when she heard the hum of a truck engine. A minute later, the doorbell rang. She looked through the glass, not recognizing the guy standing outside. "Hi, may I help you?" she said as she opened the door.

A wide smile split his face. "You don't remember me, do you?"

She took a closer look at the heavyset Hispanic guy who was about her same age. "Jorge, is that you?"

"It is."

She tipped her head. "I hardly recognize you."

He laughed in wheezy, seal-like barks, just like he had in high school, catapulting Peyton back to the past.

Jorge held his stomach. "Yeah, I've put on a few pounds since high school. But not you, flaca, you look the same as you always did."

"Thank you." Jorge had been a close friend of hers and Carter's, and he often called her *flaca*, a term of endearment that meant *skinny*. She leaned against the doorframe. "How have you been?"

"Great. You remember Lea Wilkerson from our graduating class?"

"Sort of. Are you talking about the quiet girl that sat in the back of our math class?"

"Yep." He shook his head, a wry smile forming on his lips. "But she certainly ain't quiet no more. We got married a couple of years back and have a kid on the way."

"Congratulations. It's good to see you. What're you doing here?"

"Carter asked me to stop by and drop off a gas grill. He said y'all don't have a kitchen and need something to cook on."

"Oh. That was nice." She stopped. "Wait. Do you work for Carter?"

"Yeah, technically, I work at one the wineries. But I run errands for Carter every now and again." He jutted his thumb. "I hope you like the tire swing. I put it up a few hours ago."

Peyton let out a gush of breath. "Oh, you're the one who put that up."

"Yeah, Carter asked me to. I hope that's okay." He began talking rapidly. "I knocked first, but no one came to the door. You used to have a swing there, though, so I figured it'd be okay to put one back. Is that right?"

"Yes, we did. And it's perfectly fine that you put it up." A smile stole over her lips. The tire swing had been one of her and Carter's favorite spots. It was super thoughtful of him to get Jorge to put up a new one.

"I'm going to unload the grill. Is it okay if I set it up on the patio on the side of the house?"

"Yes, that's great." She flashed a warm smile. "Thanks for all that you're doing. It was great to see you. Tell Lea I said hello."

He tipped a finger to his temple in a salute. "Will do." He turned to go, then stopped. "Oh, I almost forgot, Carter said to tell you he's finishing up a few things at the office but will be here around six."

"Thank you."

CHAPTER 13

*P*eyton's pulse picked up a notch when she heard the front door. It was six o'clock on the dot. She'd been anticipating Carter's arrival all afternoon. Her first impulse was to jump up and greet him, but she forced herself to remain seated on the couch, a casual expression on her face. "Hey," she said nonchalantly when he stepped into the living room, suitcase in hand.

"Hi, honey, I'm home," he teased, eyes twinkling.

She was unprepared for the rush of warmth that flooded her as she placed her laptop aside and stood. "Can I help bring something in?"

"Sure, that would be great. I picked up a few groceries on my way here from the office."

"Thanks. By the way, Jorge stopped by and set up the grill ... and put up the tire swing."

He went still, his eyes connecting with hers. "I hope you don't mind. I know how much you loved the other one." He shrugged. "It seemed like a good idea."

"It was super thoughtful. Thank you."

His eyes rounded slightly, like he was surprised by the compliment. Then the corner of his lip lifted in a lopsided grin. "You're welcome."

The moment got deliciously slow as Peyton's gaze discreetly flickered over his muscular, lean physique. He was wearing jeans and a black T-shirt, emphasizing his sculpted pecs and defined biceps. As usual, his hair had the perfect amount of wave. A strand had fallen in the center of his forehead, giving him a boyish, reckless look. His lips were generous but not too full—perfect for kissing. Heat pummeled over her. Where were these thoughts coming from?

He coughed slightly, an amused expression on his face as he watched her ... watching him.

She blinked. "Sorry. I'm a little slow today. Lack of sleep, I guess." An outright lie. She'd slept great, knowing Carter was in the room next door. "Let me help you get things out of the car," she said, jumping into action to hide her embarrassment.

It was the perfect evening. A slight breeze blew, and the first stars were starting to peek through the velvety sky. Peyton and Carter sat on the patio; a candle flickering on the table between them added an air of romance to the evening. A feeling of contentment settled over Peyton as she leaned back in her seat, giving Carter an appraising look. "Dinner was superb."

He grinned. "I'm glad you enjoyed it."

Carter had picked up the fixings for a green salad, along with loaded baked potatoes from the grocery store deli and then grilled salmon steaks to go with it all. Peyton hadn't realized it was possible to make such a delicious dinner without a kitchen. She cocked her head, studying him. "I don't remember you being able to cook like that before."

A smile stole over his lips. "There's quite a bit you don't know about me. It's a new day, Peyton."

"Evidently." Carter was so good-looking he nearly took Peyton's breath away. She wondered if she would ever truly be free of him. Art's advice came rushing back, and Peyton wondered if she should talk to Carter about all that had happened at the pre-wedding party.

Her heartbeat quickened at the thought, her hands moistening. The evening was going so well. It would be a shame to ruin it. Once she opened that conversation, there would be no going back. Having Carter here at the house was a tremendous blessing, and she didn't want to mess that up. Still, she needed to rip out the old before rebuilding the new.

Rip out the old ... or let things lie. Which would it be? Her tongue lay like stone in her mouth as she scrambled to find a way to give voice to her feelings.

"How did it go at Art's place?"

She let out a breath, feeling as though she'd been saved from tumbling headfirst over a cliff. "Pretty good. I got the grout sealed and the bulk of the flooring laid. When are the granite installers coming to install the countertop over the vanity base?"

"Saturday."

"Good. I'll start painting the walls and trim tomorrow. I can always do the touch-up after the installers leave."

"I'm sorry I couldn't be there today to help."

She waved a hand. "No worries. Art and I had a nice talk. He thinks the world of you."

"The feeling's mutual, I can assure you."

He just gave you the perfect lead-in for the conversation, her mind screamed. *It's now or never. Clean the wound!* She'd never had a problem with difficult conversations before. Why was this so hard? "Oh, I meant to tell you ... I'm meeting with Karen Sandburg tomorrow afternoon." Even as the words left her mouth, she was disappointed with herself for not having the courage to broach the conversation about the party disaster.

"I'll come with you."

"Are you sure? It sounds like work's crazy for you right now."

"Yeah, but I'll make time for that. It's important. How was last night? Did you hear anything strange?"

Peyton shook her head. "Not a whisper. Did you hear anything?"

"No."

She hugged her arms. "Maybe it was a fluke. But it'll be good to talk to Karen and find out what she saw and heard."

Carter nodded.

"We have an appointment with the arbitrator this coming Friday at three. Will that work with your schedule?"

He paused. "I'll have to juggle a few meetings around, but I can make it work."

"Are you sure? I can reschedule it for next week if need be."

"No, it'll be good to get that over with."

"I agree." Peyton's shoulders tightened as the old worries coiled through her. She hugged her arms. The evening was becoming chilly.

Carter surprised Peyton when he stood and went to her, holding out his hands. "Come on."

She tucked a loose strand of hair behind her ear. "Where?"

"The swing." He wiggled his eyebrows, reminding her of when they were teenagers. "Come on," he taunted. "You know you wanna." The whisper of excitement in his voice sent a flush of anticipation seeping into her cheeks. Time seemed to stand still, and Peyton got the feeling she and Carter were crossing a significant boundary as she tentatively placed her hands in his.

He practically pulled her across the yard. When they reached the swing, Carter motioned. "You go first. I'll push you."

A surge of adrenaline pulsed through Peyton when Carter stepped behind her and encircled her waist. She marveled at how right it felt to be here with him, almost like they'd been together all along.

"Here, I'll help you," he said, lifting her onto the tire. "Hold on tight," he instructed, giving her a push. Sheer exhilaration burst over Peyton as she sliced through the night air, clutching the rope. She went back and forth a few times and was about to get off and let Carter have a go at it, when he jumped on the back, his arms around her as he held onto the rope. "Woohoo!" he yelled, as they swung high in the air.

"Woohoo!" she yelled at the top of her lungs, a joyous laugh bubbling in her throat.

"Just like old times," he said softly in her ear, his warm breath tickling her skin.

A few minutes later, they got off the swing. Dizzy from the motion, Peyton plopped down on the ground. Carter sat down beside her. He lay back, placing his arms under his head, gazing up at the stars. A second later, Peyton did the same.

The darkness of the night enveloped Peyton like a protective cocoon, giving the illusion she and Carter were the only two people on earth. She was keenly aware that he was next to her, close enough to touch his hand. She balled her fist and tucked it into her side to fight the temptation. "I'd forgotten how incredibly beautiful it is here."

"Like we're getting a glimpse into countless other worlds."

"Or galaxies. It makes me feel small in comparison."

Carter angled toward her, propping his head with his hand. His lips tipped into the crooked smile she knew so well. "You could never be small. You've always been larger than life."

"Yeah, right." She smirked, turning over on her side to face him. And then she saw the sincerity in his eyes and realized he was telling her the truth.

"I've missed you," he said quietly.

She swallowed hard. "Really?" she croaked, looking at his lips, which were a mere breath away from hers. She wanted to kiss him so badly she could hardly stand it. As they moved closer to each other, a surge of panic pummeled through her, causing her to draw back. She'd fought so hard to stand on her own—to prove she could survive, even though her heart had been shattered to pieces. She didn't know if she could open herself up to Carter again.

The tiniest of smiles crept over Carter's lips. "Like I said, I missed you … I've never been able to swing like that with anyone else."

"What?" Her eyes rounded as she processed what he was saying. Then she started laughing, her mood instantly lifting as she gave him a playful shove, which sent him rolling onto his back.

"Hey, watch it!" he said, springing to his feet. He took her hand and helped her up. The air grew electric as his eyes captured hers. "Thanks for a nice evening," he murmured, leaning into her personal space.

A wave of desire rippled through Peyton. She stumbled back, but he caught her, his arm hugging her waist. A warning buzzed in her head, but she shushed it, the need to be close to Carter overtaking her good judgment. This time, when he leaned in, she closed her eyes, her lips parting expectantly.

An electric current raced through her when his mouth touched hers. His lips were soft and tentative. A tender ache pulsed through her as she drank him in, attempting to pull him closer. To her dismay, he ended the kiss abruptly and backed away. She was about to dig into him, but saw the mixture of longing and caution on his face. And it hit her—his expression mirrored her feelings. Confusion muddled her thoughts. He'd betrayed her ... broken her heart. And yet ... she got the distinct impression he'd been hurt too. She hadn't hurt him, had she?

"I'm sorry," Carter said quietly. "I shouldn't have kissed you."

She wasn't sure what to say, so she simply nodded.

"It's getting late. And we still need to clean up and take the food in."

"Yes," she said absently. "You're right. Let's go."

CARTER STRETCHED OUT HIS LEGS, his feet dangling off the end of the mattress. The antique Jenny Lind bed creaked in protest with his every movement, and he kept half-expecting it to break apart under his weight. The only way he could fit his entire body on the bed was to curl into a fetal position. The night before, he'd gotten very little sleep, partly because of the bed and partly because he'd consciously tried to remain alert so he could act quickly if anything strange happened during the night. There were plenty of other bedrooms in the house with larger beds that he could sleep in, but he sensed Peyton was more comfortable with him right next door. Maybe he should consider having a new bed delivered, or switch out one of the beds from another bedroom. But he didn't want to make waves. Peyton might freak out if she thought he was settling in for the long haul.

JENNIFER YOUNGBLOOD & SANDRA POOLE

Spending time with Peyton was both exhilarating and agonizing. More than the physical attraction that sparked like a live wire whenever they were near each other, they shared a genuine heart-to-heart connection, just as they always had. Almost as though they were a part of one another. Peyton enjoyed the same things he did. Conversation with her was effortless, and he loved her spunk. He could read her expressions so clearly that it was easy to know what she was thinking.

Well, most of the time.

She was so intoxicatingly beautiful with her expressive brown eyes and mane of thick, wavy hair. And when she smiled, her face lit up like an angel, causing his heart to swell two sizes.

The two of them were reaching a critical point. A simple friendship was never going to work for either of them. Carter could tell Peyton wanted him to kiss her tonight. And he had ... sort of. But then the doubts came rushing over him, causing him to withdraw. He was afraid if he pushed too hard ... if they moved to fast, he would lose her. He'd seen genuine fear in Peyton's eyes shortly before the kiss. What was she so afraid of?

Starting things up again with Peyton could be dangerous. She'd left him once, and he still had no idea why. Who's to say she wouldn't up and leave again?

And there was still the matter of the house. At this point, Carter was so desperate to have Peyton in his life that he didn't care if she kept her house and transformed it into a real bed and breakfast. Of course, his mother would have a cow. She'd nearly come unglued when she realized he was staying here. But as much as he loved his mother, she was far too controlling. And that was partly his fault. Carter had been so broken when Peyton left that he let his mother have full rein, mostly because he didn't care one way or the other what happened to him. And because he was worried about her health, and he didn't want to upset her. But little by little, as Carter put the pieces of his life back together, he realized he did care. All in all, his life was good, and he had much to be grateful for.

Spending time with Art had taught him gratitude. Art had more reason than anyone to be bitter about the hand life had dealt him, and he was the most appreciative person Carter knew. Art was always saying Carter had saved him, when it was really the opposite. Looking after Art had given Carter meaning and purpose.

Also, Carter got great satisfaction out of running the Webster businesses. In that regard, he was like his mother. He wanted the businesses to keep thriving, but it wasn't purely about the money. He and his mother had more money than they could spend in ten lifetimes. Carter did want to build a legacy, something he could one day leave to his own children. And like his mother, he felt it was time to build another lodge or resort, but it didn't have to be on the Kelly Property.

Carter chuckled. Maybe it was providence that Peyton's house sat in the center of his vineyards, because she'd always been the center of his greatest hopes and desires. He couldn't deny that he was still in love with her—as much now as he'd always been. For him, there'd never been anyone else. She'd brought the spark back into his life, and it would kill him if she left him again. Instinct told him he needed to find out why she'd deserted him in the first place, but he had to make sure it was the right time. If he pressed too hard, Peyton could go the other direction.

He punched the pillow, tucking it under his head. Everything was coming to a head. He could feel it building like thunderclouds on the horizon. Would he be able to persuade Peyton to give him another chance? Or would he end up losing her all over again? Maybe he was a hopeless masochist that kept sticking his hand on the hot stove, hoping this time he wouldn't get burned.

CHAPTER 14

$\mathcal{P}$eyton glanced sideways at Carter sitting beside her. He gave her an imperceptible nod, signaling her to start the conversation. She drew in a quick breath as she looked across the living room at Karen Sandburg. In her mid-sixties, Karen was a retired nurse. Her silver hair was cut in a neat bob, which fell just below her ears, and she wore very little makeup. She was dressed simply in a white sweater and jeans. Her house was modestly decorated with a hodgepodge of furniture that looked like it had come from secondhand stores. Pictures of her grown children and grandchildren hung on the walls. By all accounts, she seemed like an average, no-nonsense grandmother. Not the least bit flighty.

"Mrs. Sandburg, Carter and I appreciate you taking the time to meet with us today."

She shifted in her seat, clenching and unclenching her hands. "Please, call me Karen."

"Karen, I never had a chance to thank you for doing such a thorough job of packing up my mother and Harold's things." She flashed an appreciative smile.

Karen nodded, adjusting her sweater.

Peyton leaned forward. "Can you tell me what you saw and heard when you were working in my ... um ... the house?" Peyton amended, trying to be more cognizant of Carter's feelings. After all, the house was half his ... for now.

Karen's jaw worked, and she began blinking rapidly. There was a slight shake in her hand as she smoothed her hair.

Peyton's skin crawled with unease. It was painful to watch Karen. Whatever she'd experienced in the house had obviously shaken her up. "It's okay. You can tell us. Please ... we need to know."

Karen nodded, the lines around her mouth deepening. She clasped her hands tightly in her lap. "I was in one of the upstairs bedrooms, and I heard something." She lowered her voice, almost to a whisper. "It sounded like soft crying. I was afraid something had happened to Scott. He fell a few months ago and hurt his back. Anyway, I wanted to make sure he was okay, so I went downstairs. He was perfectly fine. I asked him if he'd heard crying, but he hadn't. I went back upstairs ..." She paused, her lip trembling. "... I was almost to the bedroom when I saw her going around the corner."

"Who did you see?" Peyton braced herself for what was sure to come. Carter reached for her hand and gave it a comforting squeeze.

"Your mother." Her voice caught. "Same hair, same height, and size." She shook her head. "I'm sorry, I know that's not what you want to hear, but it's the truth." She looked Peyton in the eye. "I swear." She shuddered, hugging her arms. "You couldn't pay me to go back in that house. And I don't think you should either."

WHEN THEY RETURNED to the car, Peyton turned to Carter. "What do you think? Is she telling the truth?"

He looked thoughtful. "That certainly seems to be the case."

"What reason would Karen have for lying?"

"None that I can see." He drummed his fingers on the steering wheel. "Who told you Karen Sandburg saw something in the house?"

"Courtney."

"Who did Courtney hear it from?"

121

"I'm not sure. She said rumors were floating around town."

"So practically the whole town knows about it."

"Yeah ... I guess. Do you think Karen really saw my mother?" Even as the words left her mouth, Peyton felt like she was asking the absurd.

"I believe she saw something." His eyes met hers. "Especially considering a similar thing happened to you."

Her eyes widened in disbelief. "Surely you don't think the house is really haunted?"

"The way I see it, there are two possibilities—either the house really is haunted ..." When she started to protest, he held up a finger. "Let me finish. Either the house is haunted, or someone has gone to great lengths to try and make you believe it is. When a practical woman like Karen Sandburg starts seeing ghosts, it lends an air of credibility to the story."

Carter had a point. Peyton tried to think. "Okay, let's rule out the first possibility. I don't believe in ghosts."

"Neither do I."

A smile touched her lips. "Well, that's a relief." Long pause. "Why would someone want me to think the house is haunted?"

"Maybe to scare you away? That's the only reason I can think of."

Her eyes locked with his, and she couldn't help but give him an accusing look. "And who would want to do that?"

He rocked back. "Are we back to this again? Surely you don't think I have anything to do with the ghost?"

"No, of course not." He looked relieved. She arched an eyebrow. "But I think you're intimately acquainted with someone who might."

He chuckled. "Like I said before, my mother's capable of a lot of things, but I can't see her hiding out in your attic pretending to be a ghost."

The thought of Kathryn Webster doing something that undignified was almost as unbelievable as the notion of there being an actual ghost in the house. "You're probably right. But someone's doing it."

"Yes ... and until we get to the bottom of it, I'm not letting you get far from my sight."

"That's awfully kind of you." She gave him a probing look. "You've dropped everything and moved into the bed and breakfast to protect me. And now you're telling me you're not going to let me out of your sight. Tell me, Carter, at the end of the day, what do you get out of all of this?"

Amusement flickered in his eyes. "Now, Peyton, don't go asking questions when you already know the answer." The air between them grew electric. "Isn't it obvious what I get?" He leaned in and trailed a finger along the curve of her jaw, his eyes caressing hers. "I get the one thing I've always wanted," he murmured.

She blinked, not sure how to answer.

He drew back, his voice growing conversational. "You hungry? I'm starved. Let's grab lunch before we head back to Art's place."

"I thought you were too busy with work to help with the renovation this week."

He shrugged. "I am busy, but as the boss, I have the prerogative of taking off whenever I wish."

"It must be nice," she said dryly.

He laughed. "Yep, it is. Very nice."

~

"THAT'S NOT GOING to do it," Peyton said, folding her arms over her chest as she eyed the bathroom wall Carter was attempting to paint.

Carter stepped back, admiring his work. "What? I think it looks pretty good."

She pointed. "You're getting more paint on yourself and the trim than you are on the wall."

He raised an eyebrow. "You think you can do better?"

"You bet I can." She reached for his brush, dipped it in the paint, and brushed a perfectly straight line along the trim. She cut her eyes to Carter. "Stick around and you might learn a thing or two."

He let out a low whistle and began clapping slowly. "Pretty impressive ... for a girl."

123

She pointed the paintbrush at him like a sword. "Excuse me? You'd better take that back … if you know what's good for you."

His eyes danced as he leaned closer. "Like I said, little girl, that was impressive. Someone taught you to color inside the lines," he taunted.

"You!" she huffed, then charged at him, intent on swiping his face with the brush. But he was faster, grabbing her arm as he maneuvered behind her, holding her arms in vice grips. "Carter. Stop!" she laughed. "What're you doing?"

"Giving you a dose of your own medicine." He forced her arm to her face, while she still held the brush. A second later, her face was striped with gray paint.

"Hey," she moaned, giggling. "That was mean."

"You want more paint?" he said, clutching her arm.

"No, no, truce!" she yelled.

"Okay, when I let go of your arms, you have to put the brush down in the tray. Agreed?"

"Agreed."

The instant he let her go, she turned and shoved the brush in his face.

"Hey!" he said, fending off the attack. "We had an agreement."

"Never trust a girl with a wet brush."

He laughed. "Indeed."

"Kids, do I need to come in there and break that up?" Art called from the other room.

Peyton sniggered. "Carter's making a wreck of your bathroom, Mr. Labrum …. I mean, Art."

"It's all her fault," Carter countered.

Her jaw dropped. "My fault? Art," she yelled, "you should see the wreck he's making of the bathroom!" Oops. Poor choice of words. Her face went hot.

"It's probably good I can't see it," Art replied good-naturedly.

Carter flashed a wicked grin. "You're cute when you blush."

"I'm not blushing," she countered, even though she knew she was. She thrust out her lower lip. "You're terrible. Look at me."

"Look at you? Look at me! I'm covered."

She laughed. "Serves you right."

He shook his head, making a clucking sound with his tongue.

"What?"

"It's not fair."

"What's not fair?"

"You look beautiful, even with paint on your face."

"Thanks," she mumbled. The heat wave that consumed her had nothing to do with embarrassment. The room felt infinitely small as Carter's eyes connected with hers.

Peyton's eyes went to his lips. Carter hadn't mentioned a word about their kiss by the tire swing, and Peyton wasn't sure how to bring it up. They were moving into uncharted territory, and Peyton was uncertain how this thing between them would end.

Carter was consuming all of her thoughts, making her crazy! The short kiss had merely whet her appetite for more. How easy it would be to fling her arms around his neck and kiss him like they'd done so many times before. A deep yearning burned through her. Her breath hitched when he touched her hair.

She tilted her head. "Do I have paint in my hair?"

"No."

Her pulse hammered in her temples as she gave him a questioning look. Her eyes ran along the line of his jaw, and before she realized what she was doing, she touched his face.

"Peyton," he murmured, gathering her in his arms.

She slid her arms around his neck. Another kiss—a real kiss, nothing held back. That's what she wanted ... for old time's sake.

"The two of you are awfully quiet," Art said loudly. "Do I need to come in there to find out what's going on?"

Peyton's eyes widened. Then she burst out laughing.

"No, that's not necessary," Carter said, shaking his head. "We're both just rolling around in paint. That man has always had rotten timing," he muttered.

"Well, look on the bright side. He can no longer send us to detention," she quipped, loving the feel of Carter's arms around her waist.

"I heard that," Art said.

"He may be blind, but there's certainly nothing wrong with his hearing," Carter grumbled, reluctantly letting her go.

Peyton sighed, reaching for a cloth. She turned on the faucet, held the cloth under the water, and then began wiping the paint off her face. "I suppose we should get back to work."

"Yes," Carter agreed, "we should."

Peyton had come within a hair's breadth of throwing caution to the wind and kissing Carter until they couldn't breathe. And while that should've freaked her out, all she could feel was disappointment that it didn't happen.

CHAPTER 15

*A*ny other time, Peyton would've appreciated the breathtaking beauty of Tiburon, the quaint coastal town just north of San Francisco. But as she and Carter walked up the steps leading to the arbitrator's home, her nerves were hammering like a renegade nail gun. Carter had been quiet on the drive, and that was fine with her, because she was consumed with her own thoughts.

Before she'd returned to Cloverdale, Peyton felt like she was finally starting to rebuild her life—gain a measure of clarity. But now she was so confused she didn't know which way was *up*. Yes, she still had unresolved feelings for Carter and would always be super attracted to him. After what she saw and heard at their pre-wedding party, she'd built Carter up to be a monster. But he was warm and genuine—the Carter she'd fallen in love with, which was more perplexing than ever.

Since their playful banter with the paint in Art's bathroom, she'd caught Carter looking at her and could sense his longing. Heck, she felt the same longing—to the very core of her being. Every time they came near one another, Peyton's skin buzzed with anticipation.

In her weak moments, Peyton imagined that the two of them might be able to start over and rebuild their relationship. But first, they would have to settle the fate of the house. And there was still

JENNIFER YOUNGBLOOD & SANDRA POOLE

Trevor to consider. His project in Texas was coming to a close, and he would be returning soon to help with the house. She couldn't have Carter and Trevor both at the house. Did she want a relationship with Trevor? She'd thought it was a possibility ... before Carter stepped back into the picture and hijacked her thoughts.

There was her show to think about, too. She'd gotten a call from her agent the day before, letting her know negotiations were nearly complete. From the way things were going, her publicist was sure there would be a season two. She took in a breath, trying to clear her head from all distractions. Right now, she needed to focus on the meeting with the arbitrator. Peyton's heart started pounding in her chest, and she felt a little light-headed. If the arbitrator sided with Carter, she would not only lose her home, but also the last tangible piece of her mother. Without warning, tears wet her eyes, and she blinked rapidly to stay them.

Concern touched Carter's features as he paused, reaching for her hands. "Are you okay? Your hands are ice cold."

"Yeah, I'm ready to get this over with."

He nodded. "Me too." Squaring his jaw, he punched the doorbell. A minute later, a heavyset man with thinning hair and glasses opened the door.

He held out his hand, shaking first Carter's and then Peyton's hand. "Hello, I'm Curtis Dunkin, Esquire." He stepped back and motioned. "Come in."

"Wow, esquire, that means he's really important," Carter whispered in her ear. Her eyes widened as she elbowed him. Carter couldn't stand it when people put on airs. Luckily, she could tell from Mr. Dunkin's placid expression he'd not heard the snarky remark.

They stepped inside. The first thing Peyton saw was an in-home oxygen device in the corner. Mr. Dunkin followed her trail of vision.

"It's for my wife," he explained. "She suffers from chronic asthma."

"I'm sorry," Peyton said.

He acknowledged her sympathy with a perfunctory nod as he led them to a study off the main hallway, where they sat down in plush leather chairs across from a mahogany desk.

Peyton's gaze took in the solid wall of bookshelves filled to the brim with books on the law. The wall on the right was covered with framed pictures of Mr. Dunkin's diplomas and myriad honors. On the wall to the left, there was a large window flanked with heavy drapes, dripping in trim. Mr. Dunkin's house was expensively decorated, albeit stodgy. She'd looked him up on the Internet, and he seemed to have a solid reputation for being impartial and thorough. Peyton crossed her legs and sat stiffly in her seat. "Thanks for taking our case," she began. "Courtney speaks very highly of you."

He leaned back in his chair, smiling. "My niece is quite the character. A very ambitious young lady, hoping to make a name for herself in the wine industry. How's she doing?"

"Great. It's been wonderful to reconnect with her. We're old friends from high school."

"Tell her I said hello."

"I will."

Mr. Dunkin cleared his throat. "Let me begin by giving you a bit of background on me. I have mediated and arbitrated numerous real estate disputes involving both residential and commercial properties. Before becoming an arbitrator, I practiced law for thirty-seven years. I received my Juris Doctor degree from Berkley." He went on for another twenty minutes, explaining in lengthy detail his experience in the field of law.

Finally, when Peyton was starting to zone out, he opened a file folder and handed both her and Carter a packet of papers stapled together at the corner. "In this instance, I'm acting as an arbitrator, as opposed to a mediator."

Peyton frowned. "What's the difference?"

"A mediator has no power to impose a resolution, other than the power of persuasion. Whereas, an arbitrator has the binding power to render a decision, as if it came from a court. If you agree to retain my services, you need to know my decision is legal and binding in the state of California."

Peyton read through the contract, relieved it was straightforward and to the point. She glanced at Carter, surprised he was watching her.

"Do you feel good about this?" he asked.

She looked at Mr. Dunkin, who wore an impassive expression as he waited for them to decide. "Yes, I do."

"Okay, then we'll move forward." Carter reached for a pen.

"Just a minute, please," Mr. Dunkin said, standing. "My secretary is in the next room. Let me bring her in to act as a notary." A couple of seconds later, a woman around Mr. Dunkin's same age came in. "This is Linda."

The woman smiled and waved. "Hello."

Carter scribbled his signature, then handed Peyton the pen. She also signed it, and they handed back their copies. Mr. Dunkin signed them both, and then Linda signed and sealed the notary section.

"I'll make you copies before you leave." He gave Linda a nod of dismissal. "Thank you." As she left the room and closed the door, Mr. Dunkin leaned back in his seat. "Would you like to speak to me privately about the case, or together?"

Peyton turned to Carter. "Which would you prefer?"

"I'm fine either way."

She thought for a minute. There was nothing Carter couldn't hear. "We can do it together, I suppose."

"Very well." Mr. Dunkin propped his elbows on the desk, his fingers forming a steeple. "So, tell me about your case."

Peyton began by telling about her mother's death and how Carter had purchased Andrea's half of the house. Then she outlined her plans for renovating the home and turning it into a viable bed and breakfast. She finished by saying how much the home meant to her because it had been in her family for three generations.

Mr. Dunkin turned to Carter. "What's your interest in the house?"

He spread his hands. "It sits in the center of my family's vineyards. I recognize how much the house means to Peyton, and I'm willing to pay her triple the value."

Mr. Dunkin looked thoughtful. "I see."

"He and his mother want to bulldoze the house and build a lodge," Peyton added, a touch of bitterness in her voice.

Mr. Dunkin reached under his glasses and rubbed his eye. "I will need to review the property details before I reach a decision. What's the best way to reach you?"

Peyton gave him her cell number. He jotted it down, then looked at Carter. "What's your preferred form of contact?"

"Through Peyton."

Mr. Dunkin looked up from his notes. "I'm sorry?"

A cocky grin spread over Carter's lips. "Peyton and I are both living at the house ... together. Just call her, and she can give me the message."

"Hmm ... an interesting turn of events." Mr. Dunkin put down his pen, wariness seeping into his eyes. "Are the two of you involved?"

"No!" Peyton blurted, her face turning blood red. She wanted to wring Carter's neck.

Amusement lit Carter's eyes. "It depends on your definition of involved. We were engaged at one time."

"A long time ago," she clarified. "We're just friends now. Carter moved into the house so I wouldn't have to be alone."

Carter wriggled his eyebrows as he looked at her. "So, friend ... you ready for our night out on the town?"

She drew herself up. "Mr. Dunkin, thanks so much for seeing us today. I look forward to hearing your decision." She gave Carter a blistering look before she turned on her heel and stomped out.

It wasn't until she got out to the car that she realized Carter had the keys. She swore under her breath and kicked the wheel of his car. Having no other choice, she stood there waiting. A few minutes later, he came bounding down the steps. When he neared the car, he waved the contracts. "You forgot your copy."

She snatched it from his hands.

"Hey, take it easy."

"How could you do that?"

"Do what?"

"Make me look like a fool in front of Mr. Dunkin," she said, her voice going hoarse with emotion. "Is this all some big joke to you?"

"No, of course not."

"Then why did you do that?"

"I was just trying to take the edge off, that's all. You looked worried, and everything was so serious."

"This is serious! This is my home we're talking about."

"I know. I meant no harm. I was just joking around."

Her eyes flashed with fury. "Well, it wasn't funny." She shook her head, feeling weary and defeated. "Can you just open the door?"

"Sure."

When they were both inside the car, Carter turned to her. "I'm sorry, I didn't mean to upset you. Really."

She nodded, her lips forming a tight line.

"So where do you want to eat dinner?"

"I'm not hungry."

His face fell. "What?"

"Can you please just take me home?"

He gave her a long look. "I said I was sorry."

"I know. But I'm tired."

He let out a breath. "Okay. Have it your way."

PEYTON HAD PUT on her pajamas and was headed downstairs to get a drink of water before going to bed, when she heard the familiar tune. She stopped in her tracks, anger exploding over her as she tromped down the stairs and into the parlor. She stood, glaring at Carter, who was pounding away on the out-of-tune piano, singing at the top of his lungs.

"'Listen to me, honey dear. Something's wrong with you, I fear. It's getting harder to please you, harder and harder each year.'"

Her brows scrunched together. "What are you doing? This isn't funny."

He laughed. "Come on, Peyton, sing it with me. You know the words."

She scowled. The last time they sang the 1920s jazz song by Irving Berlin was at the talent show their senior year in high school. They'd brought the house down and won first place.

Carter continued. "'I don't want to make you blue, but you need a talking to.'"

"I'll give ya a good talking to," she mumbled, but couldn't stop the corners of her lips from twitching.

He pointed. "I saw that. Come on, sing it with me." He grinned, looking every bit as dreamy as he had when they were teenagers.

Peyton felt her anger melting away.

"The chorus is coming up," Carter prompted.

Peyton stepped up beside him and began singing. "'After you get what you want, you don't want it. If I gave you the moon, you'd grow tired of it soon. You're like a baby. You want what you want when you want it. But after you're presented with what you want you're discontented.'"

A laugh bubbled inside Peyton, releasing the stress of the day as she sat down on the bench beside Carter. They sang the rest together. When they finished, Carter turned to her, his eyes sparkling. "We've still got it."

"More or less," she chuckled.

A wry grin twisted over his lips. "I prefer to think of it as *more*, rather than *less*."

"You're just as good on the piano as you ever were."

"And you still have a great voice." Carter nudged her with his elbow. "I'm sorry about today."

"I accept your apology."

Silence settled between them until Carter spoke. "I'm sorry we had to go through with the arbitration thing today."

She turned to him in surprise. "What do you mean?"

He sighed. "I know how much this house means to you, and if were up to me, I would just give you my half."

At first, she didn't think she'd heard him correctly. "What?"

"It wouldn't bother me if you stayed here and opened up your bed and breakfast. In fact, I kind of like having you around."

The words tumbled over Peyton as she tried to process what he was saying. "But I thought it was up to you ... you're half owner."

"Yes, that's true. But my mother's a part of this too."

"Ah, of course." Resentment spilled over her like rotten milk. It always went back to Kathryn.

"The reason I joked around at the arbitrator's office is because I couldn't stand to see you hurting. You don't know how close I came to telling him we could work it out ourselves." His expression grew troubled. "The only reason I didn't was because I promised my mother I would go through with the arbitration. When I told her I was staying at the house with you, she nearly went ballistic."

Peyton let out a harsh laugh. "I can imagine."

He gave her a lopsided grin. "My mother thinks you have this bewitching power over me. That you can make me do whatever you want. She was afraid if I came here and spent time with you, I would hand you the house on a silver platter." He shrugged. "And I would, if it were totally up to me."

Peyton's eyes grew misty.

"Hey, are you okay?" he said tenderly, brushing away a tear that escaped the corner of her eye.

She peered into the face she knew so well, getting lost in the depth of his arresting eyes that were fathomless pools of smoky gray.

Lightly, he ran a finger along the curve of her jaw, sending spirals of pleasure down her spine. The only sound in the room was her sudden intake of breath as he leaned in, cupping her face with his hands. His eyes darkened with a fierce need that matched her own as his lips touched hers. The kiss was surprisingly tender, until she let out a tiny moan and slid her arms around his neck, pulling him closer. This time, she wasn't going to let him get away. A spark ignited as she hungrily sought his lips. She'd wanted this for so long, and it was every bit as good as she remembered. Raw excitement raced over her, and she felt a burst of exhilaration mingled with a sense of belonging as their lips moved together in perfect rhythm. Finally, he pulled away, leaning his forehead against hers.

A smile quirked over his lips. "Like I said, we've still got it."

She chuckled. "I suppose we do."

"I've missed you," he murmured.

"I've missed you too," she admitted, a lump forming in her throat. Being with Carter made her painfully aware of how much she cared about him. And it reminded her of how much he'd hurt her.

He pulled back slightly, his eyes taking on a vulnerable look as they penetrated hers. "Why did you leave me?"

Irritation prickled over her. "How can you ask that when you know exactly why I left?"

"No, I don't know." A tortured expression came over him. "I've been trying to figure it out for years. Was it the embarrassment of Harold showing up at the party drunk?"

Before she could answer, his phone buzzed. She motioned. "Do you need to get that?"

"No, it can go to voicemail." His eyes held hers. "Tell me," he implored.

Either Carter was really good at acting ... like his mother ... or he didn't know. Then it dawned on her that he'd not seen her standing outside the study. He didn't realize she'd overhead his conversation with his mother or seen the girl. The painful memories cascaded over her as she stiffened.

Carter caught her arm. "Tell me."

His phone buzzed again.

Her eyes narrowed and she gave him a hard stare. "I heard everything you said to your mother that night in the study. And I saw you kiss that blonde."

Shock colored his eyes. "What're you talking about? I didn't have a conversation with my mother in the study. And I certainly never kissed a girl."

A hot anger coursed through her as she spat out the words, "Now, you're just being a jerk! Stop pretending it didn't happen. I know what

I saw." The old hurt rolled over her like a tidal wave as she scooted back from him.

He ran a hand through his hair, a befuddled look on his face. "I have no idea what you're talking about."

His phone buzzed again. He swore under his breath.

Her eyes flashed. "Go ahead. Answer it. It must be important."

He jerked the phone from his pocket. "Hello," he barked. His eyes went wide the second before his face crumbled. "What? When ... is she okay? I'll be there as soon as I can." He ended the call, a dazed look coming over him. "That was Fitz. They've taken my mother to Healdsburg District Hospital."

The fearful look in his eyes crowded out Peyton's anger as she placed a hand on his arm. "Is she okay?"

Tears gathered in Carter's eyes. "I'm not sure. She collapsed. They're running tests to see what's wrong. Will you come with me?"

She shrank back. "I don't think that's such a good idea. Your mom wouldn't be happy with that. The last thing you need to do right now is upset her."

"Please." His voice cracked. "I need you to be there."

It really was that simple. Regardless of what happened between them in the past, they needed each other. "I'll come."

He let out a relieved breath. She moved to stand, but he stopped her. "As soon as we get back from the hospital, we're going to continue our conversation. Okay?"

It was on the tip of her tongue to argue with him. What was the point of talking the thing to death? He would only deny it. But at the end of the day, she saw what she saw. And no amount of persuasion on Carter's part was going to change that. "Okay," she heard herself say.

CHAPTER 16

Ohen they arrived at the hospital, Peyton tried to remain in the lobby, but Carter insisted she go with him to see Kathryn. The lobby nurse pointed them in the right direction. A few minutes later, they were standing in front of the closed door of Kathryn's hospital room. "I really think it's better if I stay here," Peyton said.

Carter jutted his chin out, grabbing her hand. "I need you here with me." His eyes battled with hers. "Do you understand what I'm saying?"

"Yes, I just think that under the circumstances—"

Before she could finish her sentence, Carter opened the door and pulled her into the room. Kathryn was lying in a hospital bed, an IV in her hand, and hooked up to a heart and blood pressure monitor. She was still as beautiful as always, with her perfectly applied makeup and dark hair spilling over the pillow. But she looked frail. A joyous expression came over her face when she saw Carter, but that look changed to something venomous when she realized Peyton was standing behind him. Fitz was sitting in a nearby chair. He acknowledged Carter's presence with a curt nod.

Carter approached the bed and gave Kathryn a tight hug. "How are you?"

"Better now," she said haltingly.

Carter turned to Fitz. "What happened?"

"The preliminary test results are showing anemia. If her red blood cell count doesn't rise in the next few hours, they'll give her a blood transfusion."

"Did the tests show anything else?"

Kathryn chuckled dryly. "Only that I have leukemia." She patted Carter's hand. "You don't need to worry about me. It'll take more than anemia to do me in."

"I see you haven't lost your sense of humor." He kissed her forehead.

Not knowing what else to do, Peyton just stood there. As if the look Kathryn gave her wasn't bad enough, she could tell from Fitz's stern demeanor that she was not welcome. She straightened her shoulders. She was here for Carter, and that's what counted.

Carter seemed to remember then that she was there. He stepped back and put an arm around her waist. "Mom ... Fitz ... I asked Peyton to come with me." There was a hint of defiance in his voice as he eyed them both.

Fitz just looked at her, but the change in Kathryn was instantaneous as a cherubic smile spread like warm butter over her lips. "Peyton, darling, it was so good of you to come and see me. Carter tells me you're doing a great job on Art Labrum's renovation."

Peyton got the feeling she was watching an award-winning performance, delivered by a seasoned actress. "Thank you. Carter's been a big help as well," she said woodenly.

Carter gave her a look of pure adoration. "No, it was all Peyton."

Silence descended over the room, until Kathryn spoke. "Well, it was very kind of you to come with Carter tonight. Don't you agree, Fitz?"

Time seemed to stand still as Fitz's cool eyes appraised Peyton. "Yes," he finally said, although it seemed to pain him to say it.

A chill went through Peyton. Fitz was an odd duck.

They stayed another fifteen minutes or so, until Carter said, "Well, we should get going." He took Kathryn's hand. "Please be nice to the doctors. Do what they say, okay?"

A crease appeared between her brows. "Of course. I always do," she quipped.

Carter was amused. "Fitz, please make sure she follows orders."

Fitz raised an eyebrow. "I'd just as soon tell the sun to rise at a different time each day."

A giggle escaped Peyton's throat, but it was snuffed out instantly when she saw the look of pure hatred on Kathryn's face which was almost immediately replaced with a benevolent smile. "Take care of yourself, dear."

"Thank you," Peyton mumbled.

"See, that wasn't so bad," Carter said when they stepped into the hall and closed the door. "There may be hope for you and my mother yet."

"Yeah ... maybe." Peyton doubted Kathryn would ever accept her, but there was no sense in throwing that in Carter's face. He was worried sick about his mom, and Peyton didn't blame him.

"Thank you," he continued. "I really appreciate you coming here with me tonight."

The sincerity in his eyes shot straight to the center of her heart as a bubble of warmth burst over her. "You're welcome," she said softly.

WHEN THE DOOR CLOSED, Kathryn turned to Fitz, fire sparking in her eyes. "This has gone on long enough. Peyton must be dealt with ... immediately!"

He titled his head, studying her. "But I thought your plan was working."

"It is," she snapped, but not fast enough. "And even when we get control of the house, it still may not be enough to eradicate Peyton from Carter's life. You saw how he looked at her tonight." Tears pooled in her eyes. "After all the trouble I went through to get rid of her ... and now they're together again." She snapped her fingers. "Just like that."

Fitz stroked his chin. "One could argue that they really love each other."

"Love's a poor substitute for the cold, hard facts of life." Her face hardened. "Carter's my son, and I plan to save him—even if that means saving him from himself. Get rid of her. I don't want her coming back this time."

He nodded. "I'll take care of it my way. And I can guarantee there won't be any loose ends."

~

THE MINUTE they stepped inside the front door, Carter pulled Peyton into his arms and gave her a long kiss that left them both breathless. He took her hand and pulled her to the sofa. "Okay, now we get to finish our conversation."

Peyton ran a hand through her hair, which felt stringy and unkempt. She was so tired she could hardly think straight. The last thing she wanted to do was get into a verbal sparring session with Carter. One minute she was flying high on the emotional see-saw and the next she was plummeting to the ground. "Do we really have to talk about this tonight?"

His jaw tightened. "Yes, you accused me of kissing some girl on the night of our party. I demand a full explanation. Tell me what you saw."

She hesitated, feeling as though she were opening Pandora's box. Even the very room in which they sat seemed to be holding its breath, waiting for her to continue. Pain simmered in her eyes as she began telling him about the night forever seared in her memory. "We were on the stage. Harold showed up and made an idiot of himself. I went to the restroom to put myself back together.

"When I came out, I went to find you. As I was walking past the study, I heard voices."

He cocked his head. "The study? Why were you back there?"

"Someone was in front bathroom, so the maid escorted me to the one by the study. The French doors were open. There was a catering cart parked beside the doors. I got as close as I could. I heard everything as clearly as if I'd been standing beside you." Her eyes hardened. "You and Kathryn were in the study. You were sitting in a chair, with your back to me. Kathryn was standing. She was furious about Harold wrecking the party. She said she'd never been so humiliated in her life. And then she told you it would never work between us because we came from two different worlds. She said you felt obligated to me and that you were too good-hearted to end things."

An incredulous look came over him. "What? That's absurd."

"Don't deny it," she snapped. "I saw it." Her voice broke. "I heard you tell Kathryn she was right. That you didn't love me anymore. That you felt sorry for me but were so far in that you didn't know how to get out." Tears rolled down her cheeks. "Kathryn assured you it would be okay. Then she said she had a surprise. Your true love had flown in from New York to see you." Bitterness rose in her throat. "The blonde came in. When you saw her, you let out a whoop ..." A sob escaped Peyton's throat. "... and the girl rushed across the room into your arms. So I left, and didn't look back." That last part wasn't exactly true. The whole time Peyton was running away, she was looking over her shoulder, focused on the past. But she wasn't about to admit that to Carter. She let out a cleansing breath. As painful as it was to rehash the memories, Peyton was relieved it was finally out in the open. She looked at Carter. "Well, say something," she said softly.

He rubbed his neck, a stunned expression plastered over his face. "I'm not sure what to say."

"Maybe you can start by apologizing. Admitting what a louse you were. Tell me how you made the biggest mistake of your life when you let me go." She bit her lower lip to keep it from trembling.

He looked her in the eye. "I would tell you all of those things, except ..."

"Except what?" she demanded.

He threw his hands in the air. "It never happened."

"Of course it happened. Stop denying it. I saw it," she said hotly.

"I never went into the study. Don't you remember? I was going to go with you to the restroom, but Fitz pulled me aside, asking questions about security protocol and how to handle the situation with Harold. I stayed outside with the guests, waiting for you to come out." He rubbed a hand across his forehead. "I've never felt for one minute that you and I were a mistake. There was no blonde from New York. I love you, Peyton. I've always loved you."

"Stop it," she barked.

Desperation touched his features. "Stop what?"

"Stop trying to rewrite the past to suit your whims."

He shook his head. "Are you sure you didn't imagine the whole thing? You were distraught over Harold. Maybe your mind was playing tricks on you. Did you have anything to drink?"

"You know I don't drink." She jumped to her feet, a crazed look coming into her eyes. "It happened! Just as I described." She balled her fists. "And if you really love me, you wouldn't try to make me believe it didn't." She turned and ran up the stairs, slamming her bedroom door shut and locking it.

CHAPTER 17

*P*eyton sat up in bed with a groan. Her head pounded like she'd been clubbed. After the argument with Carter, she'd thrown herself on the bed and cried herself to sleep. What a disaster this whole thing was turning out to be. Just when she thought she and Carter could make a go of it, everything blew up in her face. Before coming back here, memories of Carter had dulled enough to ebb the pain. Now everything was fresh. She could still feel his lips on hers. See his cocky grin. How his face would light up when he laughed. The admiration in his eyes as he watched the transformation on Art's bathroom. She raked hair from her face, holding it in a ponytail behind her head. No more wretched thoughts about Carter. She reached for her phone. Yikes! It was nine-forty. She couldn't remember the last time she'd slept this long. Carter was an early riser. No doubt he'd been up and gone since six.

Today, they were supposed to install fixtures in Art's bathroom. Unable to find a single decent-looking light fixture in the surrounding stores, Peyton ordered them from a trusted design supplier out of Texas. They'd arrived yesterday. She and Carter were going to install them today. Once the granite installers did their part tomorrow, the job would almost be done. And that was fine with Peyton. The less time she spent with Carter, the better.

She jumped in the shower and let the hot water run over her shoulders, soothing her aching muscles. As she was applying her lipstick, she glanced at her phone and realized she'd missed a couple of calls from Trevor. She reached for her phone to call him back, when it buzzed with an unfamiliar number.

"Hello."

"Miss Kelly, this is Curtis Dunkin. I wanted to let you know that after spending the bulk of the day reviewing your case, I've reached a decision."

Her heart began to pound and she felt shaky. "Yes."

"There's really no easy way to say this, so I'll get right to the point. While I understand and appreciate your emotional attachment to the house, I am of the opinion it's in the best interest of the parties involved that you sell your half of the home to Carter, in the which he will pay you triple the market value."

The air left her lungs. "No!" Tears rushed to her eyes. "You don't understand. This house is all I have left of my mother."

"I know this is difficult, and I assure you, I did not reach my decision lightly."

She gripped the phone as a wave of dizziness overtook her. Mr. Dunkin continued droning on about the legal aspects and how he would have his secretary send over the paperwork regarding his decision, but she barely heard a word.

"Miss Kelly, are you there? Hello?"

A curious numbness settled over her as she ended the call. She gulped, her breath coming in ragged gasps. Then came the splintering anger. She dropped her phone, slumped down on the floor, and wept.

CARTER WASN'T sure what to make of the strange story Peyton had told him. He mulled it over the entire night, hardly getting a wink of sleep. It was obvious Peyton believed what she was saying. The whole thing felt like an eerie repeat of the conversation he and Peyton had with Karen Sandburg. Was the whole world going nuts?

On an upside, he'd gotten a call from Fitz telling him all the tests had come back, and the only thing showing up was his mother's anemia. That was reassuring. Her doctor instructed that she be given a blood transfusion shortly after he and Peyton left the hospital. According to Fitz, his mother had more energy than she'd had in months. She'd checked out of the hospital early that morning and was at home resting. Carter planned to visit her later in the day, but there was one stop he had to make first—Art's house. Art was one of the most level-headed people Carter knew. Hopefully, he could shed light on the situation with Peyton.

"Is Peyton here with you?" Art asked the minute Carter stepped through the door.

"No, she was still asleep when I left. I assume she'll come over later."

A smile touched Art's features. "It seemed like you were getting along great the other day. I thought I was going to have to send you back to detention." He paused, cupping a hand behind his ear. "What, no laughter? I thought that was passably funny. What's going on?"

"Do you mind if we sit down?"

"Sure."

They went into the living room. Carter began the minute they got seated. "Peyton and I had a big argument last night."

"That's to be expected. Anytime two strong-willed people come together, there's bound to be friction. I'm sure you'll make up."

"Peyton was acting really strange."

Art's forehead creased. "How so?"

Carter told him all Peyton had accused him of at their party. Art made him repeat the story three times, asking details. Then Carter told him about the house and how Peyton had heard crying, then laughter and found her mother's ring on the dresser. He even repeated the conversation they had with Karen Sandburg. "There never was any other girl at the party. I was thrilled to be marrying Peyton. She's the love of my life," he added, his voice catching. "What do you make of all this?"

"Let's take it one piece at a time. First of all, Peyton's as honest as the day is long. If she says she saw you in the study talking to your mother, then I believe her."

Carter's face fell. "Are you saying I'm lying?"

"No, you're also honest."

Carter rubbed a hand through his hair. "You're not making any sense. One of us has to either be lying or delusional, and I can assure you it's not me," he huffed.

Art held up a hand. "Take it easy. There are several things about Peyton's story that strike me as odd. Peyton didn't use the guest bathroom because it was occupied. Then a maid took her to another bathroom in the back of the house near the study."

"Yeah."

"Did she say what the maid's name was?"

"I didn't think to ask her." Carter shook his head. "My mother brought in a whole staff of people to help with the party."

"According to what you said, Peyton only saw you from the back … from a distance. Is that correct?"

"Yes, there was a catering cart, parked by the door, preventing her from getting closer."

Art held up a finger. "Ah, a catering cart was blocking the way. A coincidence? Or was it put there for a reason?"

Carter jerked. "Are you saying the whole thing was staged?"

"It's a reasonable assumption. It wouldn't have been that difficult for someone with the right skills to pull it off. Lots of people look similar from behind, and if they're wearing the same type of clothing …"

Carter's blood started pumping furiously as he scooted forward, rubbing his hands on his jeans. "Do you think my mother did this?"

"She's an actress. She knows other actors and actresses. Peyton saw Kathryn's face, but only the back of your head. Kathryn led the entire conversation. That's the only scenario I can come up with, other than Peyton imagining the whole thing. And I don't think she did."

The words were a succession of hard punches that left Carter feeling breathless. The whole thing was so unbelievable ... and yet, he couldn't deny that it made sense. His lips grew thin with anger as he looked at Art, who was staring vacantly back at him. "Do you think my mother would stoop that low?"

Art gave him a sad smile. "Do you really want me to answer that?"

A sickening disgust rankled Carter's gut. If his mother did this, then she was the reason he'd been estranged from Peyton all these years.

"Your mother loves you, and I'm sure that somehow she has twisted this thing around in her mind, convincing herself she did you a favor."

"She ruined my life!"

"No, she didn't ruin your life. She only delayed your happiness by a few years. You and Peyton are together now."

"We were starting to come back together, but I didn't believe her when she told me what happened. I accused her of being distraught, imagining the whole thing."

"I take it that didn't go over well."

He chuckled darkly. "No."

"Which explains why you're here talking to me rather than Peyton."

Carter moved to stand, his eyes narrowing into slits. "It seems like I need to have a talk with my mother."

"Yes, but first we need to discuss the other piece of the puzzle."

"The other piece?"

"The strange things that have been happening in the house."

Carter's head shot up. "Do you think my mother's behind that too?"

"Well, I certainly don't believe it's a ghost. And someone's doing it. If Kathryn went to the trouble of staging the scene at the party, then it's probable she would attempt to make Peyton believe the house is haunted to scare her away."

A hard edge came into Carter's voice. "Well, there's only one way to know for sure. It's time I had a talk with my mother."

~

WHEN CARTER GOT to the mansion, there was an unknown car in the circular driveway. He let himself in the front door and went down the hall. He was walking in the direction of his mother's bedroom, when he heard voices from her study. The French doors Peyton had spoken of had long since been replaced by a sliding barn-style door. The door was three-quarters of the way closed. Carter's first reaction was to slide the door open and barge in. Instead, he paused, craning his ear to hear. He heard his mother and another voice he didn't recognize. Ever so slowly, he peeked around the door, looking through the gap. His mother was talking to Courtney.

Courtney spoke first. "I'm sorry to bother you when you've just gotten home from the hospital, but I couldn't wait to share the good news."

Kathryn dismissed the apology with a flick of her wrist. "Nonsense. I'm fit as a fiddle. And I could use a bit of good news."

"My uncle came through with flying colors. The Kelly Bed and Breakfast is now yours ... or at least it will be, once the paperwork goes through."

Carter stiffened, feeling the urge to punch something.

"That's fantastic," Kathryn said. "You can tell your uncle I'll wire the money to the account number he gave me."

"That'll be great. He could really use the money. My aunt has been sick for a long time. The medical bills are stacking up."

"Well, that was part of the deal," Kathryn snipped. "I'm happy to know his exorbitant price is being put to good use."

"Um ... about the rest ... it wasn't easy making Peyton think the house was haunted. I would've done more, had Carter not moved in ..."

"Yes, as agreed, I'll make you the marketing director over the

148

wineries. But you're never to mention a word of our agreement. Is that understood?"

"Absolutely."

At this point, Carter had heard enough. He shoved the door open and stepped in. Courtney nearly jumped out of her seat when she saw him, and Kathryn's pallor turned the color of death as she clutched the arms of the chair.

"How could you?" Carter looked at Courtney. "Peyton considers you a friend."

Courtney's face blotched an ugly red as she stood and lifted her chin high in the air. "Yeah, that was apparent when she deserted me." She glowered at Carter. "You should be thanking me. The Kelly Bed and Breakfast will no longer be an eyesore, and you'll be able to build your lodge. Kathryn, if you'll excuse me ..."

Kathryn gave her a dignified nod, like a queen dismissing her servant. "Of course."

When she'd gone, Carter turned to his mother. "So you orchestrated the whole arbitration thing. Unbelievable."

"I did what I had to," she muttered, leaning her head against the back of the chair. "This is not a good time," she said weakly.

Carter sat down in the same seat where Courtney had been. "That's interesting, considering you just told Courtney you were fit as a fiddle."

Kathryn's head snapped. "Don't get insolent with me."

Carter leaned forward, his jaw set in stone. "I'm going to ask you something, and if we're going to ever have a prayer of rebuilding our relationship, then you'd better tell me the truth."

Kathryn began blinking rapidly. "What're you saying?" She wrung her hands. "I—I don't understand."

"Cut the bull, Mother." His voice cracked like breaking ice through the room, causing Kathryn to go still.

Her face puckered into itself as she sat up straight in her chair. "Okay," she said in a normal voice. "What is it?"

"The night of my pre-wedding party ... in this very room. Did you act out a scene with someone pretending to be me? Did you hire a blonde to rush in and kiss me?"

"What?" she exclaimed with a laugh. "That's ridiculous."

But for a split second, before the actress could take control, Carter had seen a glimmer of fear in her eyes. The knowledge hit him like a sledgehammer. He gasped. "You did, didn't you?" He thought of something else as the pieces clicked into place. "When Harold showed up at the party, he was mumbling about getting a check. You got him to come to the party. Probably had someone get him drunk. And then you had an actress, pretending to be a maid, direct Peyton to the bathroom off your study."

Kathryn put a shaky hand to her throat, fingering her pearl necklace. "I would never do something like that."

Carter just sat there, looking at her. He had the feeling none of this was real. How could his own mother do something so sinister? Something that hurt him so deeply.

Indignant tears glimmered in her eyes. "How could you accuse me of such a thing?" She grabbed a tissue from her desk and used it to dab her eyes.

He didn't change his expression a fraction.

"Stop it!"

"Tell me the truth," he demanded through clenched teeth. "Tell me!" he thundered.

She flinched, something breaking loose in her eyes. "You want to hear the truth? Fine! Yes, I did it. It wasn't that hard to pull off. Peyton's so utterly predictable."

Tears burned Carter's eyes as the hurt sliced through him. "You ruined my life!"

"Oh, quit being so dramatic. All Peyton wanted was to get her claws into you so she could get the money." She clenched her jaw. "My money."

A blinding fury cut through Carter. "Peyton never cared about the money."

"Of course she cares about the money," she flung back. "That's all she's ever cared about."

"Did you ever stop to think she might have loved me?" He put a balled fist to his chest, his voice hitching. "She loved me and I loved her." He gave her a scalding look. "You're pathetic, Mother."

A wild look twisted her features. "How dare you say that me? All I've ever tried to do is protect you. I did what I had to, because you couldn't see it." A smug look came over her. "But you know what? None of that matters now. Fitz is taking care of Peyton. And it's my sincere hope that she'll stay out of our lives this time!" She stopped, her eyes rounding as she realized what she'd said.

An icy fear snaked around Carter's heart. "What did you say?"

"Nothing."

He sprang from his chair and grabbed her arms, shaking her. "Tell me! What did you do?"

CHAPTER 18

$\mathcal{A}$fter Peyton's tears were spent, she stood and rinsed her face in the sink, staring at her reflection in the mirror. How in the heck was she supposed to give the house up? Her phone buzzed. Trevor ... again.

"Hello."

"Peyton, I've been trying to call you all morning."

"Yeah, I've been a little busy," she said dully.

"I've got great news! We got the contract for season two. We start filming in January."

"That's great," she said, fresh tears brimming in her eyes.

"I'll be finished with my project by the end of the week. I'll fly back there, and we can make great strides on the bed and breakfast remodel before we start filming."

"Yeah, that's not gonna happen."

"What?"

Emotion choked through her as she tried to speak.

"Peyton, what's wrong?"

"I lost the house," she squeaked.

"What do you mean?"

Somehow, she managed to voice the words. "Carter and I went to an arbitrator and he ruled in Carter's favor. I have to sell him my half of the house."

He hesitated. "I'm sorry. Can you contest the decision?"

She ran a hand across her forehead. "I don't think so. It was my idea to see the arbitrator." She gulped. "The crazy part is that Carter told me he would've given me his half of the house had it not been for his stupid mother." Anger stirred within her as the words gushed out. "You know what? That was probably just a big lie. Carter never had any intention of giving me his half of the house. When he moved in here, I thought he was being nice, but he was probably playing me the whole time."

"Whoa ... hold it. Carter moved in?"

"Yeah, but only because he was worried about me being in the house by myself."

Long pause. "You love him."

Peyton swallowed. Oops. She'd not meant to tell Trevor about Carter moving in, but it was too late to recall the words. The damage had been done. She could hear the hurt in Trevor's voice.

"Do you love him?" he asked.

She squeezed her eyes tightly shut. "No, I don't love him," she barked, pounding her fist on the dresser. "I hate his stinking guts. I trusted him! And he hurt me all over again."

"I see."

"What's that supposed to mean?"

He let out a breath. "Look, Peyton, I'm not sure what's going on with you. But whatever this is ... you don't need me in the middle of it. The best thing I can do is give you space to sort it out. When you're ready to come back, I'll be here."

She didn't know what to say. It wasn't fair to lead Trevor on. And he was right. She did need space to figure this out. "Yeah, you're probably right," she heard herself say, trying to squeeze back tears. "I'll call you in a day or so."

"Okay." Long pause. "Peyton, take care of yourself."

"Thanks," she squeaked, ending the call. A deep sadness settled over her like it had when she'd dropped Trevor off at the airport. But this time, there was no question. There would never be anything romantic between them.

She jumped when she heard what sounded like footsteps in the attic. A hysterical laugh rose in her throat. "Not again," she grumbled.

Clutching her phone in one hand, she threw open the bedroom door and looked both ways down the hall. This time, she was not going to be quelled by some imaginary ghost! She tromped down the hall and stomped up the steps leading to the attic. "Whoever you are, I'm coming for you," she said loudly. "Did you hear me? I'm not afraid of you. The house's going to be torn down anyway. What's the point of haunting it?" She opened the door and stepped inside, feeling a measure of relief that no one was there. She laughed at herself, her shoulders relaxing. Then she heard a sound from behind. Before she could react, she heard a loud whack and simultaneously felt a blinding pain. She fell to the floor, darkness overtaking her.

~

PEYTON COUGHED. Her head felt big and sore, and her lungs were on fire. She gulped, trying to get air, but there was only smoke. She sputtered as a coughing fit overtook her. She blinked and moved slightly, feeling the hard floor beneath her. Then she touched her head, which was sticky.

Confusion swirled around her as she sat up, wincing in pain. She looked over and saw the flames bursting from the curtains and cardboard boxes. Everything came rushing back as she let out a strangled cry. Someone had followed her to the attic and hit her over the head. The window had been boarded over, preventing her escape. She turned and tried to open the door, but it was locked. Acrid smoke was billowing around her. She crouched to her knees, staying low to the floor as she felt around for her phone. But it was nowhere to be found.

Was this how it was going to end? She gulped, trying to breathe as she covered her mouth with her T-shirt. She knew she needed to do something—fast! But she felt sluggish and slow. Memories from her childhood overtook her. She saw her mother's face. Felt her comforting embrace. Then an image of Carter flashed through her mind. Despite everything, she did love him. The certainty of her feelings surged through her with a cruel irony. She was finally realizing her feelings, when it was too late. Art's words rang through her head: "Not a one of us is guaranteed a tomorrow." She uttered a silent prayer, *Please, help me.* Dizziness overtook her.

She heard a crash, followed by a whoosh of fresh air. The next thing she felt were strong arms gathering around her ... lifting her up. And then she was floating.

～

"Peyton, can you hear me? Peyton! Wake up!"

Peyton blinked, then coughed. Her eyelids were as heavy as cement, and her head ached.

"Look at me."

Reluctantly, she opened her eyes as Carter's face came into focus. They were on the ground in front of her house, and he was cradling her in his arms, his face streaked from tears and soot. "You're okay," he cried, pulling her close. "Thank God, you're okay."

She looked up at him. "You saved me."

Then she heard sirens. Alarm raced through her as she clutched his arm. "The house."

"I called 911. The fire department is on its way."

Tears pooled in her eyes. "Someone came from behind and hit me over the head."

His jaw tensed, his expression livid. "Fitz."

"What?" With some effort, she managed to sit up.

Carter kept a protective arm around her. A tortured look came over him. "You were right about everything. My mother orchestrated the whole thing. Everything you saw at our party happened, just as you said." He paused. "Except it wasn't me. My mother hired a double to act as me. And then she placed the catering cart in the way so you couldn't get too close."

Peyton gasped. "Are you serious?" She thought back, her mind racing through the sequence. "I tried to move the cart, but it was stuck … but I saw you."

"You saw someone that looked like me from behind. Had you gotten closer … and not been so distraught, you probably would've noticed something was off."

Her mind grappled with what he was saying. She shook her head. "The blonde girl?"

"An actress my mother hired."

Her lips started to quiver, as the implication of what he was saying tumbled over her. "How could I have been so stupid? All this time I thought you betrayed me."

He put both arms around her, a fierce look in his eyes. "I would never betray you. I love you."

She thought back to the realization she'd had just before she passed out. The certainty she felt. Warmth covered her like a protective blanket. "I know that now. I love you too."

A new light settled in his eyes. "You do?"

She laughed. "Yes, Carter Webster, I do." Tears glistened in her eyes. "I've tried to convince myself I can live without you. And I proved to myself that I can."

His face fell. "Oh."

A smiled tugged at her lips as she touched his cheek. "But I was absolutely miserable in the process."

He chuckled. "Me too. We belong together."

"Yes, we do."

He sighed heavily. "I wish we could just leave it at that, but unfortunately, there's more."

When he hesitated, she gave him a tender look. "Tell me, please."

"My mother was working with Courtney. The whole arbitrator thing was a setup. My mother was able to bribe Mr. Dunkin because he needs money for his wife's medical expenses."

She gasped. "That's why Courtney recommended him."

He nodded. "Courtney was the one trying to make you believe the house was haunted. I'm sure she figured when the arbitrator ruled in my favor, you would be all too happy to leave this place behind."

"Courtney? Are you sure?"

"I heard it from her own lips."

Peyton felt like she'd been slapped as the hurt of betrayal splintered over her. "I thought Courtney was my friend."

"I think she was … at one time. Unfortunately, she never got over the fact that you left."

"So Courtney did all of that out of spite?"

"Not entirely. My mom promised to make her the marketing director for the wineries."

"I see," she said, her lips forming a tight line. "What're we going to do about your mother? She tried to kill me," she said hoarsely.

His eyes took on a wounded look. Then he grew resolute. "She'll have to pay for what she's done. And so will Fitz."

"But what about her leukemia?"

"I don't know," he said, shaking his head.

"Hey, look at me," she commanded.

His eyes met hers. "What?"

"We'll figure it out together, okay? If the two of us could find our way back together despite all the obstacles that have been thrown in our paths, I'm sure we can figure this out. Art was right—we have a magic that most people can only dream of."

He grinned. "Did Art say that?"

"Yes, he did."

"Remind me to thank him later," he murmured, drawing her close. The familiar passion enveloped them as he gave her a long, slow kiss.

EPILOGUE

*T*en months later ...

A sense of déjà vu wafted over Peyton as she stood in the courtyard at the Webster Mansion, almost in the very spot she'd stood years earlier at the pre-wedding party. It was a warm evening, just as it had been then. She smiled nostalgically as the delicate scent of fragrant flowers kissed her senses. White lights twinkled against the onyx sky, reminding Peyton of diamonds against black velvet. Music from the live orchestra floated in the air. The scene was almost the same as it had been before, but vastly different in the way that counted the most. She was different. No longer the timid girl playing dress-up at the ball, Peyton was all grown up.

Season two of her show had just wrapped. It had been grueling to spend so much time away from Carter, even with frequent weekend visits. But it wasn't the same as being together all the time. Going back to Texas had given Peyton the perspective she needed to know it was time to make some significant changes in her life. For Peyton, there wouldn't be another season of *Fix It Up*. She would have to find a way to break the news to Trevor, but she knew he would understand. He might even be relieved. It had been difficult for Trevor to see her with Carter. But in the end, they remained good friends, which is all they'd ever been to start with.

Peyton was itching to resume renovating her house. A smile played on her lips—her and Carter's house, she amended. They were still co-owners. At this point, Peyton wasn't sure if she wanted to turn it into a bed and breakfast, or just live in it. The fire had done a doozy on the house. There was much work to be done. She frowned. Thinking about the fire brought back thoughts of all that had happened.

Peyton hadn't seen Courtney since she learned what her supposed friend had done. Peyton didn't care if she ever saw Courtney again. Unfortunately, she couldn't say the same for Kathryn. Peyton looked up at the windows facing the courtyard, wondering what Kathryn was doing at this very moment. Fitz was in prison for attempted murder. But because of Kathryn's medical condition, her influence, and because she swore up and down that she had no idea Fitz was going to try and burn down the house with Peyton in it, Kathryn's sentence was reduced to house arrest. Peyton had seen Kathryn only a handful of times since the fire. The older woman was cordial, but kept her distance. Peyton couldn't imagine that she and Kathryn would ever be able to mend their relationship. However, because they both loved Carter, they would need to find a way to coexist.

Peyton frowned. She must've gotten her times mixed up. Carter had asked her to arrive at six, and it was already six-fifteen, but she was the only one here. It seemed strange to be alone amidst such grandeur, with only the members of the orchestra playing, as if a crowd of people were listening.

Her breath caught when Carter stepped up behind her and encircled her waist. "You look stunning," he murmured in her ear. His lips moved like a feather down her neck, sending titillating thrills circling through her.

She turned to face him. He looked sharp in a black suit and white button-down shirt. Her eyes trailed to his open collar as a smile tipped her lips. "What? No tie? That's not like you."

He grinned. "What can I say? I'm a rebel."

She laughed. "So it would seem."

He slipped an arm around her waist and pulled her so close she caught a hint of peppermint on his breath. "So, the filming is done?"

"Yes."

"Excellent. You're all mine now," he said, passion darkening his eyes.

Warmth radiated through Peyton as she smiled. "Yes, and you are mine."

"Dance with me," he said, swaying to the music.

"So, where is everybody?"

Rather than answering, Carter twirled her around and dipped her back over his arm, gazing into her eyes. "Everybody's here." He lifted her up.

"What?"

"This is it."

A surprised laugh bubbled in her throat. "You did all of this ... for me?"

"Yes," he said, his eyes shining. "This time, I wanted to do things right." Her eyes widened when he got down on one knee. "Peyton Kelly, there's something I need to ask you." His beautiful eyes searched hers. "Will you marry me?"

Her heart leapt with joy as tears rushed to her eyes. "Yes," she exclaimed, laughing and crying at the same time. "Yes!"

He stood and pulled her into his arms. "I love you, Peyton." He chuckled. "I was a goner from the first minute I laid eyes on you."

"I love you too," she said softly.

Their lips connected. In Carter's tender kiss, Peyton found the promised hope of many tomorrows to come. She had finally come home.

CLICK HERE to get your copy.

GET YOUR FREE BOOK

Hey there, thanks for taking the time to read *Love Under Fire*, a companion book to The Hawaii Billionaire Series. If you enjoyed it, please take a minute to give me a review on Amazon. I really appreciate your feedback, as I depend largely on word of mouth to promote my books.

Love Under Fire is a stand-alone novel, but you'll also enjoy reading the books in The Hawaii Billionaire Series. Be sure to check out the continuation of Trevor Spencer's story in Love at the Ocean Breeze

Love Him or Lose Him

Love on the Rocks

Love on the Rebound

Love at the Ocean Breeze

Love Changes Everything

Loving the Movie Star

If you sign up for our newsletter, we will give you one of our books, Beastly Charm: A contemporary retelling of beauty & the beast, for FREE. Plus, you'll get information on discounts and other freebies. For more information, visit:

http://bit.ly/freebookjenniferyoungblood

BONUS CHAPTER OF LOVE AT THE OCEAN BREEZE

Lacey's stomach growled. If only she'd thought to pack a granola bar ... or something to snack on. She and Milo had been trudging through the overgrown trail for over an hour. She'd drained her water bottle in the first twenty minutes of the hike, and a blister was forming where the strap of her sandal rubbed relentlessly against her heel. *Why had she not thought to wear tennis shoes?* "Can we please turn around and go back?" she asked wearily.

Not bothering to look at her, Milo waved a hand as he increased his pace. "The waterfall's great, babe. There's a pool below it where we can swim. We're almost there. Just a little further."

"That's what you said thirty minutes ago," she grumbled, hurrying to keep up. Milo had grown up in the nearby town of Hauula, Hawaii. But he hadn't been to this waterfall since he was a kid. Even though he swore he knew the way, Lacey was starting to wonder. At this point, she didn't give a flying flip about some waterfall—no matter how beautiful it was. But Milo was determined to forge on until he found it or they passed out from exhaustion. And judging from the way things were going, it would most assuredly be the latter.

Lacey swatted the mosquito on her leg. She managed to kill that one, but ten more took its place in the blink of an eye. She was getting eaten alive! The air oozed moisture, bathing her in sticky sweat. If only her Texas friends could see her now. She glanced at the waist-high weeds and vines growing in tangles, and the trees crowding in around them. It looked like a scene straight out of *The Jungle Book*. She chuckled humorlessly at the thought. She'd come to Hawaii three months ago on vacation. Her second day on the island, she met Milo Kahele at Waimea Bay where he was back diving off a cliff. He was a local boy—a surfer heartthrob with a quick smile and great body. They'd been inseparable ever since. Her older brother Trevor didn't approve of the relationship and would freak if he knew she was living with Milo. Trevor was always calling and texting, trying to get her to come back home and enroll in a community college. But it was none of his stinking business what she did with her life. She was an adult and could do as she pleased. She had no intention of sitting in a boring classroom. She'd never had as much fun with anyone as she had with Milo … well, most of the time, present activity excluded. Her lips formed a petulant scowl. If Milo didn't find the wretched waterfall soon, she was going back to the house—with or without him.

Milo stopped so suddenly that Lacey nearly toppled forward to avoid barreling into him. "Careful," she growled.

Milo stepped into a clearing, and Lacey followed close behind. For a split second, she thought he might've actually found the waterfall, but no—it was only a crummy building that looked like it had been forgotten eons ago.

"I could've sworn we were going the right way," Milo said, scratching his head.

"Obviously not," she retorted, blowing out a long breath. "We need to go back. I have a blister on my foot." She looked at her heel. It was bleeding. Where was a Band-Aid when she needed it?

His shoulders sagged in defeat. "Okay."

Lacey plopped down on the ground. "I need to rest a minute before we head back." She groaned. It felt good to sit down. "Care to join me?"

"Yeah," he said absently, his eyes darting to the shack. "A strange place for a building."

"I guess." Lacey stretched out her legs, her stomach growling again. "Do you have any snacks in your backpack?"

"No, sorry. I think I'm gonna check it out."

Her face fell. "What? The building? No." She pointed. "There's a padlock on the door. That's code for *keep out*."

"Nah, dat means there's something valuable inside."

"Yeah, spiders and bugs."

He wriggled his eyebrows, an adventurous smile curving his lips. "Be right back."

"I don't think that's a good idea," Lacey said, but he was already jogging towards the building.

Milo tugged on the padlock. When it didn't budge, Lacey assumed he'd grow tired of the game and come back. To her dismay, Milo found a rock and beat on the lock. A couple of minutes later, it broke. Milo pushed open the door and stepped inside.

Lacey tensed, glancing around. Even though it looked forgotten, the building belonged to someone. And the owner certainly wouldn't appreciate Milo breaking into it. Milo was a daredevil from the word *go*, which is what attracted her to him. But this was going too far. She stood.

"Milo," she called, "you've had your fun. It's time to go."

No answer.

"Milo!" she said angrily, rushing toward the building.

Before Lacey got to the door, Milo came running out, a look of exhilaration on his face. "You won't believe it. The whole building's filled with crates of paintings and statues."

"Whatever's in there, doesn't belong to us. We need to go."

He let out a loud whoop. "Ever heard of *finders keepers*? This is incredible, babe." He took her hand. "Come on. I'll show you. The stuff looks expensive."

Lacey picked through the crate closest to the door. It didn't take a trained professional to know that Milo was right. The paintings were exquisitely done in vivid detail. The items were valuable.

"We can sell these." He began talking fast. "One piece will probably

165

bring more money than we could make in a year." He laughed. "Ten years." He clenched a fist. "Oh, my gosh. I can't believe it!"

"I don't know." Lacey chewed on her cheek. "These pieces belong to someone. They'll come back for them. Maybe they're stolen."

Milo grabbed her arms, a feverish excitement in his eyes. "There aren't any car tracks leading to the building. And the lock was so old and rusted that all I had to do was barely hit it and it fell off. This is our lucky day. Think about it," he said enticingly. "No more waiting tables, for you. We can eat at the best restaurants. Stay in nice hotels. Maybe even buy a house."

It was tempting. Everything in Hawaii cost a fortune. Lacey had blown through her meager savings in the first week and had taken a waitress job at a café, which paid barely enough to cover her food and other expenses. Thankfully, Milo was letting her stay at his place rent free, but that couldn't last forever. Eventually, she'd have to start paying her fair share. And she couldn't do that on what she was making now. "But what'll happen if somebody finds out we took these things?" A shudder ran through her as she glanced around, looking for cameras. "What if the place is under surveillance?"

He nodded. "You're right. We need to be careful. I have a friend we can call. Someone who can help."

"A friend?" She shook her head. "I dunno. Maybe we should just walk away and pretend we never found this."

"Turn our backs on a fortune?" He squared his jaw. "We'll never get another chance like this." His eyes battled hers. "Please? Just let me call my friend."

"Okay," she finally said.

A smile broke over his lips. "You won't regret it. We're gonna be rich!"

Continue Reading

ALSO BY JENNIFER YOUNGBLOOD

Check out Jennifer's Amazon Page:
http://bit.ly/jenniferyoungblood

Billionaire Boss Romance

Her Blue Collar Boss

Her Lost Chance Boss

Georgia Patriots Romance

The Hot Headed Patriot

The Twelfth Hour Patriot

The Unstoppable Patriot

O'Brien Family Romance

The Impossible Groom (Chas O'Brien)

The Twelfth Hour Patriot (McKenna O'Brien)

The Stormy Warrior (Caden O'Brien and Tess Eisenhart)

Rewriting Christmas (A Novella)

Yours By Christmas (Park City Firefighter Romance)

Her Crazy Rich Fake Fiancé

Navy SEAL Romance

The Resolved Warrior

The Reckless Warrior

The Diehard Warrior

The Stormy Warrior

The Jane Austen Pact

Seeking Mr. Perfect

Texas Titan Romances

The Hometown Groom

The Persistent Groom

The Ghost Groom

The Jilted Billionaire Groom

The Impossible Groom

Get the Texas Titan Romance Collection HERE

The Perfect Catch (Last Play Series)

Hawaii Billionaire Series

Love Him or Lose Him

Love on the Rocks

Love on the Rebound

Love at the Ocean Breeze

Love Changes Everything

Loving the Movie Star

Love Under Fire (A Companion book to the Hawaii Billionaire Series)

Kisses and Commitment Series

How to See With Your Heart

Angel Matchmaker Series

Kisses Over Candlelight

The Cowboy and the Billionaire's Daughter

Romantic Thrillers

False Identity

False Trust

Promise Me Love

Burned

Contemporary Romance

Beastly Charm

Fairytale Retellings (The Grimm Laws Series)

Banish My Heart **(This book is FREE)**

The Magic in Me

Under Your Spell

A Love So True

Southern Romance

Livin' in High Cotton

Recipe for Love

The Second Chance Series

Forgive Me (Book 1)

Love Me (Book 2)

Short Stories

The Southern Fried Fix

ABOUT THE AUTHOR

Jennifer loves reading and writing clean romance. She believes that happily ever after is not just for stories. Jennifer enjoys interior design, rollerblading, clogging, jogging, and chocolate. In Jennifer's opinion there are few ills that can't be solved with a warm brownie and scoop of vanilla-bean ice cream.

Jennifer grew up in rural Alabama and loved living in a town where "everybody knows everybody." Her love for writing began as a young teenager when she wrote stories for her high school English teacher to critique.

Jennifer has BA in English and Social Sciences from Brigham Young University where she served as Miss BYU Hawaii in 1989. Before becoming an author, she worked as the owner and editor of a monthly newspaper named *The Senior Times*.

She now lives in the Rocky Mountains with her family and spends her time writing and doing all of the wonderful things that make up the life of a busy wife and mother.

For more information:
www.jenniferyoungblood.com
authorjenniferyoungblood@gmail.com

www.jenniferyoungblood.com

facebook.com/authorjenniferyoungblood

twitter.com/authorjenn1

instagram.com/authorjenniferyoungblood